OVER

GONE – BOOK THREE

Stacy Claflin

To receive book updates from the author, sign up here.
http://bit.ly/1ONrfMw

Alone

HEATHER SQUIRMED AGAINST the tight restraints. The jacket wouldn't budge. She tried to readjust her right shoulder because the jacket pinned her in the most uncomfortable angle. Pain shot through her arm in all directions.

How had she come to this? She was a normal sixteen year old—or she had been until everything crumbled around her. Her dad had killed her mom. Why wouldn't anyone listen to her? He needed to be locked up, not her.

She stopped fighting the straight jacket and found that her arm didn't hurt so much. She needed a new plan. So far, nothing else had worked. That much was obvious. Heather looked up at the camera in the ceiling.

They were watching her, those sadistic nurses. How they were able to keep their jobs, she would never know. If she ever got out, she'd tell everyone what really went on. But she didn't know how she would ever get out. She had turned into the problem patient and they were intent on fixing her.

How long would they keep her in seclusion this time? Time moved slower than ever in there, so she never could tell. Didn't they know they were making her crazy? Or maybe her dad paid someone off to torment her so she appeared to go off the deep end.

Sure, attacking the head nurse hadn't been her best moment, but Heather hadn't seen any other options. No one would listen to her. She had tried convincing them of her mental health, tried to make them listen. But no, they had to keep pushing her. It should have been no surprise that she snapped.

Heather had already gone through enough with losing her mom, but then to be locked away like a criminal? They took her for observation, at least that's what they told her. The fact that her dad didn't visit her should have told them something, but it hadn't.

Where was that jerk, anyway? He must have been enjoying the time to himself. Or could he be on the run because of what he had done to her mom? Heather doubted that, because if anyone knew he had killed her, Heather wouldn't be locked up.

Instead, she suffered their torture while trying to deal with the fact that her mom was never coming back and her dad was responsible. Anger burned within the pit of her stomach. She wanted to scream and kick herself free. Not that it would get her the attention she wanted. She would only get more time in solitary.

She fought to free herself from the jacket again. More pain shot through her shoulder and arm. Tears ran down her face. They probably laughed at her from behind the camera.

They had sent her into the room to punish her, and now with her in tears it was icing on the cake. They won and she lost. She stared into the camera, imagining the icy-cold eyes of the head nurse.

Finally, the tears stopped and she looked away from the camera—her only link to humanity. How long had it been since she had had real contact with people? Not the people inside the building, but her friends at school. Did they miss her? If they did, why hadn't anyone come to see her?

More tears stung, but she blinked them away. What waited for her outside the walls? Anyone? Did anyone care that she languished inside a nut house, turning into someone who belonged there?

Maybe if someone would have bothered visiting her, she wouldn't have found herself going down this path. Or if any of the nurses bothered to be nice to her. That would have gone a long way. But no, they taunted her instead. Just like they were doing now.

If she could push her anger aside and ignore the injustices, would that help? If she pretended as though the cruel witches were actually human beings with feelings? Would that help?

The thought of being nice to them sent chills through her. It would be like admitting defeat, or worse, saying what they had done to her had been okay. On the other hand, if it was a step toward getting out, it might be worth it.

Heather took a deep breath and thought about her grandparents and their farm. It had been so long since she had been out there. She had missed going there for Christmas break. There was nothing like Christmas on the farm. She even had her own room there, even though it wasn't how she would have had it. She would give anything to see them.

She closed her eyes and imagined being in the kitchen with Grandma, making some soup. She loved to make it from scratch, and nothing else compared to it or anything she made. Her mouth watered as she actually smelled the soup. In the background, she heard Grandpa's old sitcoms. He probably knew each episode by heart, but that didn't stop him from watching them over and over.

It had been so nice to visit them, even though she knew it wasn't real. At least not yet. She would get back there. Heather had no other option. Next she pictured her home, but it sat empty. She tried to draw up images of Mom, but she was still gone. Tears escaped Heather's closed eyes. How would she get through the rest of her life without her mom? Especially since her dad had gone off the deep end?

She had to get out of the mental hospital. Even if it meant sucking up to the nurses. She knew she wasn't insane. Anyone living through what she had to endure would act up, too.

Heather took a deep breath, and prepared what she would say. She opened her eyes and stared into the camera. The words fought to stay inside. She didn't want to say them, but she had no other choice. "I'm sorry. I shouldn't have hit that nurse."

Waiting

THE WIND HOWLED, pushing on the light tent. Coyotes howled in response, not too far in the distance.

Macy Mercer wrapped a blanket around herself, shuddering. "They don't sound so far away this time."

Allie shook her head, pulling her own blanket tighter. "I hope the guys are okay."

"They are." Macy sounded a lot surer than she felt. She looked into Allie's scared, green eyes. "They know what they're doing, and when they come back, we'll have a nice meal too."

Another animal howled, but this time midway through it let out a high-pitched yelp. Barking followed.

Allie moved closer to Macy, who opened up and wrapped her blanket around the younger girl.

Tina sat up across the tent. She looked around. "What's going on?"

"The boys went to get food," Macy said. "They wanted us to have protein."

"That wind won't give up." Tina moved her long, light brown hair out of her face. "You think Jonah's looking for us in this weather?"

"Wouldn't surprise me," Allie said. She shook in Macy's arms.

Macy held her tighter. "We've barely stopped in the last two days. Even if they are looking, we have such a good head start I don't think it matters."

Tina pulled her hair into a ponytail. "Yeah, but they have vehicles. We don't."

"They can't get cars through these woods," Macy countered. "We've all got cuts from those thorn bushes."

"Horses. They have horses."

"You think they could get horses through some of those paths?" Macy ran her hand along a scab that went from almost her eye down to her lip. "There's no way."

Tina narrowed her eyes. "They have things to cut away shrubbery. Jonah's the most determined man I've ever met."

Allie sniffled, making crying noises.

"Maybe we should talk about something else," Macy said. "We're scaring Allie."

"She should be scared—we all should be. That's what's going to keep us going, and keep us alive."

"We should be aware, sure," Macy said. "Not scared, though. That's not going to help us. We've made it this far, with so little food and sleep. Then we found this abandoned camp site."

"All the more reason to be afraid."

Macy raised an eyebrow.

"Did you stop to think why all this stuff was abandoned?" Tina asked. "People don't generally leave a tent full of blankets unless something's wrong."

"Maybe one of them got hurt, and they didn't have time to pack up. They just left to get to a hospital."

Tina ran her hands through her ponytail. "Whatever you want to tell yourself. I'm going back to sleep." She tucked herself into the sleeping bag, covering her head.

"Do you think she's right?" Allie asked.

"I think she has the right idea of going back to sleep. We need our rest."

"Can I sleep in your bag with you?"

"Sure." Macy reached over and pulled Allie's pillow over and then unzipped her sleeping back and connected the two.

Before long, Macy listened to the sounds of both the other girls' heavy breathing along with the wind whipping the tent. Was Tina right? Would Jonah and the others use horses to catch up to them?

It didn't seem likely. They didn't know what direction the group of kids had gone, and they probably assumed they went to the highway.

Macy had wanted to go there, but Luke said that would be the first place they looked.

They had been on the run for more than two days. It would be difficult for them to find the group of kids. They were at the base of the mountains, so the woods went for miles in every direction. How would they know where to start looking?

No. Luke had meant it when he told Macy that he was going to help her get back home to her family—her real family. Not with Chester and Rebekah. If Chester got his hands on her again…Macy shuddered.

She would fight him to the death. He had kidnapped her once, but it wasn't going to happen again. She'd been stupid enough to get into his truck in the first place. Since then he'd starved her, beaten her, tied her up and left her imprisoned…but the worst part was being away from her family for so long. It nearly ripped her heart out. Macy had wanted independence for so long—but not like this.

The wind whipped the tent, lifting one side from the ground. Macy sat up a little, listening for the guys. She couldn't hear a thing beyond the wind and the occasional animal in the distance. They seemed to be moving farther away. Was that good or bad? If they were leaving because they sensed something bad was going to happen, then Macy needed to be prepared for whatever that was.

At least all of the camping gear belonged to someone else. If it was destroyed or they had to leave it behind, it wouldn't matter. No one had any attachments to it.

The longer the boys were away, the more Macy's stomach twisted. She couldn't push away images of bad things happening to Luke. The thought of Chester getting a hold of him…it was too much. Maybe he was strong enough to fight him off. Unless Chester had his gun on him, then it might not matter.

Macy hadn't heard any shots, so that had to be a good sign. She couldn't do anything about it, and what she really needed was more rest before they moved on. Despite her worries, she closed her eyes and tried to relax her mind. There were five guys out there. They'd be able to handle themselves.

As she listened to the wind and the sounds of the other two girls' breathing, Macy found herself drifting off. Part of her wanted to fight it, but she gave in.

Conversation awoke her. She felt rested; how long had she been sleeping? Sitting up, she noticed the wind had stopped. Tina wasn't in the tent, but Allie still slept next to her.

Macy slid herself out of the sleeping bag, trying not to wake the younger girl, but she stirred and rubbed her eyes. "Is it time to get up?"

"I think the boys are back. You can sleep if you want. We'll probably eat and keep going."

"No. I want to go with you." Allie sat up and stretched.

Macy tried to fix her hair, but gave up. They all looked ragged after being in the woods for a few days. Half of them had dirt caked on their arms or face, and everyone's white clothes were dirty.

The two girls grabbed their shoes and put them on before exiting the tent. Tina sat by the campfire with the guys. Relief washed over Macy when she saw Luke. He smiled when he saw her and Macy threw herself into his arms. He squeezed her.

"What took you guys so long?" she asked.

"The wind scared a lot of animals into hiding, but we did find that guy." He pointed to something roasting over the fire. It looked like it had been a fox. "I'm not sure that it'll fill us all, but at least it's more substantial than berries."

Macy's mouth watered. The irony didn't escape her, and she wondered if she would ever go back to being vegan.

"Did you get rest?" Luke kissed the top of her head.

"I did. Don't you need some?"

"What I need is something to eat. My stomach hasn't stopped rumbling."

"How much longer until it's ready?"

"It hasn't been cooking long. Want to go for a walk?"

She stared into his eyes. "Are you sure you don't want to sit and relax?"

He took her hand, sliding his fingers through hers. "What I want is to spend some time with you while we're not on the run." He turned to a couple of the others and told them they wouldn't be gone long. He led her into the woods where there was barely a path.

"How much longer do you think until we reach the end of the woods?" Macy asked.

"I wish I had an idea. Just as long as we get there."

"What are you going to do when we reach civilization?"

He squeezed her hand. "Help you get back to your family."

"After that?"

"I'll figure something out. We need to tell the authorities about the community. There are other kids in there against their will, taken from their families. Maybe my mom will leave and we can find a home together, but I'm not counting on that. She's really happy there."

They came to a boulder, and Luke sat. He indicated for her to sit too. She did and he wrapped his arm around her. "I'm almost eighteen, so I'll probably find myself a job. I'll manage."

"Without a real education? I mean, I know you've been in school, but I don't think the community lessons will count for anything."

"You worry too much."

"No I don't. You need—"

"We have to focus on getting out of the woods first. Then we can—"

"If you're under eighteen, you could get a foster family and then go to high school. You could catch up and even graduate."

He held her closer. "I'll do that. Okay?"

"You're just saying that."

"Maybe."

"So, what's your real name? You never did tell me. Everyone else is going by them except you."

"I've grown to like Luke."

"You were going to tell me in the corn fields. Remember?" Macy asked.

He was quiet for a moment. "I was, wasn't I? Lucas is actually my middle name, so even though I changed my name, I've still held onto a piece of myself."

"Did you go by that before the community?" asked Macy.

"If I tell you, will you keep calling me Luke?"

"Sure, but you have to tell me. Otherwise, I'm going to have to make up something." She turned to look at him. "You look like," she paused, "a Walter."

"Walter?" Luke laughed. "Really?"

"Yeah," Macy teased. "If you don't tell me your name, I'm going to call you Walter."

"I'm definitely not Walter. Looks like I need to tell you."

"You should...Walter."

Luke shook his head. "My first name is Raymond."

"Raymond? You don't look like a Raymond."

"You'll let me stick with Luke?"

"Luke it is."

He ran his fingertips underneath her chin and placed his lips on hers.

Macy's heart pounded against her chest, and before she had time to react, Luke pulled back. "We should rejoin the others."

Pursuit

LUKE AND MACY walked back to the camp hand in hand. Everyone was sitting around the campfire.

"What'd we miss?" Luke asked.

"We're just trying to figure out how much longer until we're out of here," Tina said.

"It's got to be a ways," Luke said. "There are no sounds of anything other than wildlife. We have to plan for the worst."

"What's the worst?" Allie asked. She shivered.

"A week, maybe more," Tina said.

"No." Macy shook her head. "The worst would be Jonah and Chester finding us."

The others all said their agreements.

"How's the fox look?" Luke asked.

Trent poked it with a stick, moving it around. "It actually looks pretty close."

"Good," said Luke. "We should look around the camp and see if there's anything we need to take with us."

Most everyone dispersed, going through the two tents and the other random stuff left behind by the previous inhabitants.

"Why do you think they left without their stuff?" Macy asked.

Trent poked the fox again. "Could be anything, but I've learned not to question a good thing."

"You don't think we need to worry?" Macy asked.

He shook his head. "If they were coming back, they would have already. Could have been a storm or wildlife that chased them off. Who knows?"

"Too bad they didn't leave us a car," Luke said.

Trent laughed. "That would've been helpful."

"I don't even see any tire tracks," Macy said.

"That's not surprising," Luke said. "It's been so windy. We were lucky to find the tents still standing."

Macy stood closer to the fire to warm up while Trent and Luke discussed the best options for getting out of the woods. She half-listened to them while letting her mind wander back to her family.

She'd been gone at least a couple months. Did they still hold hope for finding her alive? Had Chester sent them any more messages? He had posted her fake status saying she ran away and then he left her bloody clothes. Did they even think she was trying to get to them?

Tears filled her eyes. If they could just get back to civilization, she wouldn't have to wait much longer to find out. She thought about them for a little while longer until everyone else gathered back around the campfire.

Trent looked at the fox again. "Looks good enough to eat. Let's dig in. Anyone find a knife?"

Allie held up a rusty pocket knife. "It's kind of gross though."

Luke took it. "Thanks, Allie." He opened it up and held the blade into the flame. "This will kill any germs."

Before long, they were all cutting off pieces. Macy was surprised that everyone was so generous—making sure that others had some before digging in. They all had to be as hungry as her, but they probably weren't used it. Between Chester starving her and her self-starvation before that, she could handle the hunger—not that she was going to turn down the food.

Her mouth watered as she held the warm meat in her hands. Macy looked at it for a moment, holding onto the smell before finally digging in.

After everyone had some, Trent and Luke handed out seconds. The portions weren't as big, but the animal was down to the bones after that. Allie and Tina brought some berries they had collected and everyone passed those around.

Macy pulled closer to the fire as she finished the berries. It felt good to have food in her stomach again. That coupled with the sleep, she felt that she could go on until they got out of the woods.

"Should we stay another night or get going?" Trent asked.

"As much as I'd like to stay where we have a camp," Luke said, "I don't like staying in one place. Jonah isn't one to give up easily. We need to move on."

Trent looked disappointed, but nodded. "You're right."

"Why don't you take a nap?" Macy asked. "You guys were gone hunting for a long time. Get some rest."

"I think I will." Trent got up and went into the tent the guys had slept in.

Luke wrapped his arm around Macy. "Are you cold?"

"It feels like it's going to snow."

He sniffed. "Smells like it too."

Macy giggled. "You can smell snow coming?"

"You can't? It always has that smell right before."

Macy sniffed. "Yeah, I guess I can smell something different in the air."

"That's snow." Luke pulled her closer. "You know what I think?"

"What?"

"There's going to be—"

Loud rustling noises sounded not far away. Luke jumped up, grabbing the pocket knife from the side of the fire.

"What's that?" Macy whispered.

Luke put a finger to his mouth.

Macy stood up. Everyone looked around, wide-eyed and silent.

Another rustling sound.

Blood drained from Macy's face. She didn't know if she was more scared of a wild animal or Chester. Either way she could end up dead, but Chester knew how to torture. She scooted closer to Luke.

Trent came out of the tent. He grabbed a large stick and held it up.

More rustling noises. This time they were closer.

"Found them! Over here!"

Jonah.

The sounds of hooves and more rustling noises came from the same direction.

Kids around the camp screamed.

"Run!" yelled Trent.

They went in different directions. Luke grabbed Macy's hand and pulled her in the opposite direction as Jonah's voice. She fought to keep up. Her heart pounded in her ears and she had a hard time getting her feet to do what she wanted.

Luke led her through thick bushes where the leaves scratched her face as they ran. There was no path and they kept running into trees and other plants blocking their way.

Macy heard a high-pitched scream followed by Allie's voice screaming no.

A strange sound escaped from Macy's throat.

"We have to keep going," Luke said.

"What are they going to do to Allie?"

Luke held a pricker bush out of the way. "Hopefully just a public shaming. Come on."

"Shouldn't we try to help her?"

"I promised to get you back to your family. Let's go."

Macy moved around the pricker bush. "But she's so young."

Luke pulled on her hand and they ran through a tight path. "I know, but from the sounds of those hooves, there's too many of them. We wouldn't be able to fight off the prophets. Jonah probably has half the men from the community."

"I feel horrible about leaving them."

"Chester is undoubtedly after you. If anything, they're using the others as bait to draw you in. You don't want to fall into his trap, do you?"

Images of being locked under Chester's barn flooded her mind. "No. We have to go."

Luke squeezed her hand. "There's nothing we can do to help the ones the prophets catch, but I can protect you and get you back home."

Macy's throat closed up. All of this was her fault. If she hadn't gotten into Chester's truck in the first place, none of this would have ever happened. She wouldn't have been taken, he wouldn't have tortured her. Now all these other people were going to be hurt. She couldn't get Allie's face out of her mind. "I hope Allie's going to be okay."

"Her parents are assistant prophets. I'm sure she will." Luke's tone didn't sound as sure as his words.

"I hope so."

They ran in silence for a few minutes and then more screams could be heard from the direction of the camp site. Macy couldn't tell who it was, but it sounded like at least three. Were she and Luke the only ones to escape?

Luke turned and gave her a sympathetic look, but didn't slow down. They kept running, passing through tight paths, getting scratched along the way. Not that it was anything compared to whatever the other kids were going to go through.

He squeezed her hand. "Hurry up, Macy."

Before long she was gasping for air.

"Do you need to slow down?" asked Luke.

"I don't think we can, can we?"

"If you need to, we can stop."

Her lungs burned and her mouth was parched.

"Maybe just for a minute."

Luke stopped, also taking deep breaths. "We're probably okay for a few minutes, but we'd better run again as soon as we can."

In between gasps, Macy said, "It's getting dark."

Luke looked up. "We should have another hour of light."

"Then what?"

"We should keep going as long as we can."

Macy's stomach twisted in a tight knot. She felt like she was going to throw up, but she was determined to keep the food down. Who knew when she would be able to eat that much again?

"Are you ready?" Luke asked.

Tears filled her eyes.

Luke's expression softened. "Don't cry."

Her lips wavered. "I can't help it. I'm so tired of everything. I don't want to keep running."

He pulled her close. "You have to. We're close. I can feel it. It's always darkest before the dawn. Just keep going a little farther. Can you do that?"

Macy blinked and the tears fell to her face. "I have to. I can't go back to Chester."

Luke kissed her cheek. "Don't think of that. Think about getting back home. You probably have your own room. What do you have in there?"

"All my stuff. Everything."

"Think about that. Come on." He caressed her palm and then slid his fingers through hers. "Ready?"

Macy took a deep breath. "Guess I'm gonna have to be."

Luke looked into her eyes. "You are." He tugged on her hand and they were off and running again.

Tears flew through the air behind her. Macy couldn't help it. She was tired and didn't know if she had the energy to keep going until they hit civilization.

Found

"WE SHOULD TAKE a break," Luke said.

It felt like they had been running for days, but it had only gotten dark a short while before. "Okay." The moon shone bright, helping them to see as they ran.

Luke smiled, slowing down. "Not going to argue?"

Macy shook her head. Her legs burned. "Is your leg okay? You hurt it in the corn field, and we haven't stopped except for last night."

"It hurts a bit, but I'm fine."

She squeezed his hand and then pulled away from his grip. Macy rubbed her hand. It ached from being in the same position the entire time they ran. "Are we going to sleep here?" She looked around, not seeing anything that looked appealing. Rocks and thorn bushes mostly.

"Do you have a better idea?"

"Not really. I wish we had a place to hide."

"If we sit by that rock we'll be somewhat hidden by the bush."

Macy squinted. "Probably."

Luke sat against the rock and held out his arm. She sat next to him and he wrapped his arm around her. "At least we can keep each other warm. That's not so bad is it?"

A smile tugged at Macy's mouth. "No. I can't complain about that."

"We should take turns staying awake. You get some sleep first."

"But I slept while you were hunting that fox."

"You're not going to sway me, pretty thing. Close your eyes and get some rest. You're going to need it."

"So are you."

"I'll wake you, and then it'll be my turn. Close those eyes."

"Yes, sir," Macy teased. She closed her eyes and leaned her head against his chest. She pushed her face against it, noticing his muscles.

She listened to his heartbeat as he told her a boring story in a soft, soothing tone. Before long, her eyes grew heavy, and she gave into sleep.

"Macy."

"Mph."

"Macy, wake up."

She sat up. "Is everything okay? Did they find us?"

"No," Luke said. "You mind sitting up while I sleep?"

"Of course. You need your sleep." She yawned.

"Here, take this." Luke handed her a thick stick. "I've been sharpening it with the knife. We can use it as a weapon if we have to."

"Okay. Do you want me to work on one while you sleep?"

"If you want. We can't have too much protection." Luke handed her the knife. "We can use that, too." He leaned his head against her shoulder.

She kissed his hair. "Get some rest."

He snored.

"I'll take that as a yes." She held up the knife and looked for another stick. There was one just out of reach. She used her feet to pull it to her, not wanting to disturb Luke's rest. She grabbed it and slid the knife along the edge, pointing away from her.

She worked on the stick until it had a sharp point. After finishing, she slid the three weapons in between her and the tree they sat against.

Macy listened to Luke's heavy breathing and felt sleepy herself. She couldn't allow herself to sleep.

Her eyelids grew heavier. She sang a song in her head, trying to distract herself. She had to stay awake.

A branch snapped nearby. Macy sat up, holding her breath. Her heart pounded in her ears, making it hard to hear. She tried to calm herself. If she wanted to survive, she needed to stay alert.

Another branch snapped. Macy looked around. A fat raccoon darted in front of her. She let out a sigh of relief.

Everything was quiet for a while, and to keep herself from falling back asleep she thought about what she would do when she got back home. First she would hug everyone and apologize profusely. She would swear never to sneak out again—and she would keep the promise. Then she would let Alex tease her all he wanted, and then when he ran out of things to say she would run down to Zoey's house and find out what she'd missed.

She found that she couldn't even think about her parents, beyond apologizing to them. She'd been gone so long. What must they be going through? She shook her head, a lump forming in her throat. No. She'd cried enough already. More than enough. Macy needed to be strong to get back home.

If they wanted to ground her for life, Macy would have no qualms. She just needed to get out of the woods.

The thought of that was enough to wake her and get rid of the sleepiness. She'd never have to be locked away under the barn again or stuck in a crazy cult, locked inside there too. Being grounded at home with people who loved her would be freedom compared to everything she'd been through recently.

A noise caught Macy's attention. It sounded pretty far away, and she couldn't tell what it might be. She sat a little taller, slowly sliding her hand behind her where she'd put the weapons. Her fingers wrapped around one of the sticks.

She heard another noise, this time closer. It sounded like rustling leaves. Could it be a breeze? She didn't feel anything, but there could be a wind somewhere else.

Another branch snapped. Could it be a raccoon again? Her skin crawled, starting from her back and moving down to her legs. She sat up taller, ready to wake Luke if she needed to. She didn't want to wake him over a forest animal.

More leaves rustled, this time closer and louder. It sounded larger than a critter. They needed to move on.

Macy couldn't find her voice, so she elbowed Luke. He moved his head, but didn't wake. She nudged him again, this time harder. He didn't respond.

She scanned the area, still not seeing anything. Her pulse was on fire. She'd have to find her voice if they were to get away. She heard another rustle.

"Luke," she whispered. "Wake up. Something's headed our way."

He sat up, looking around. "What? Where?"

"That way." Macy pointed. A branch snapped loudly as if to prove her point.

"Where's the knife?" Luke asked.

Macy pulled the knife and other stick out from behind her.

Luke took the knife, leaving her with both sticks. He stood up, pressing his back against the tree. Macy did the same.

"We need to go the direction we came," whispered Luke. "Follow me."

Macy nodded. Luke headed toward the tiny path they had taken, and she hurried to keep up. They made it a few yards before Macy stepped on a branch. It snapped with a loud crack. She cringed. "Sorry."

"We have to hurry." Luke grabbed her hand and pulled her though the path.

They darted between bushes, trees, and thorns. Macy's hair kept getting caught in the thorns.

"There you two are."

Macy's heart stopped.

Chester.

Luke pulled Macy. "Keep going."

She forced her feet to move faster, but she was all too aware of Chester behind them. She couldn't let him catch them. Macy held the two sticks in her hand tighter.

Macy felt a hand on her shoulder. She turned around and screamed, regretting it immediately. If the prophets were out there searching near Chester, she had just informed them of their location.

Luke tugged her arm again. Though Chester had touched her shoulder, he hadn't managed to grab her.

It wasn't over...it was just beginning. They were going to get away from him.

They had managed to lose him in the corn field, and they could do it out here. It would be easier, because they had wide open spaces. They weren't locked inside the community.

Macy tried to kick dirt behind her as she ran. It probably wouldn't do anything to slow down Chester, but she had to do something.

"Where are you going?" Chester called. "We need to talk, Heather."

"Her name's not Heather," Luke yelled without looking back.

Macy picked up her speed and got right behind Luke. She could feel the material of his shirt on her face.

"You're headed for a nest of mountain lions," Chester warned. "Turn around and live, Heather."

"What?" Macy exclaimed.

"He's lying," Luke said. "Keep going."

"No, I'm not," Chester said, sounding closer. "There's a whole group of them. Turn around."

"You turn around," Macy said. "We'll take care of ourselves. Go back to Rebekah."

"Not without you. We're a family."

Macy let go of Luke's hand. She stopped and turned around and stopped. "We aren't a family. We've never been a family. I'm not Heather, and you know it. You ripped me away from my real family."

Luke grabbed her hand and pulled her away. "Don't let him get to you."

Rage built up in the pit of Macy's stomach. "I can't help it. I've never been able to tell him how I feel."

"Write him a letter when he's in jail."

Macy felt Chester's hand on her shoulder again. This time, he squeezed and pulled her toward him.

Done

C HESTER HELD MACY, his glasses gleaming in the moonlight.
"How did you fix your glasses?" she asked.

"Fix them?" He laughed. "I keep a spare set because I need them so desperately. Now come with me, Heather. We have some matters to discuss."

Her blood ran cold. She wanted to look back at Luke, but didn't dare take her eyes off Chester. She tried pulling away from him. His hand slipped, and she ran in the opposite direction, feeling thorns scraping her on all sides.

She heard Chester muttering over the sounds of her and Luke's running. Each time she brushed against foliage, it made noise. Her senses were overwhelmed and she didn't even have time to process anything.

Chester wasn't far behind and he was yelling at her to slow down and give up, still calling her Heather. When would he give up that delusion?

Macy kept turning and running, trying to keep up with Luke. Her legs burned even worse than before, but she didn't let that stop her.

Eventually, she was sure that they had lost Chester.

Macy slowed down, breathing heavily. Even that burned, just like everything else. Luke turned and looked at her, appearing out of breath, too.

She stopped and put her hands on her legs, trying to catch her breath. Had they actually lost Chester? Even if they had, they needed to keep going.

She thought she heard something come her way, so she jumped up, grabbed Luke's hand and ran. She brushed past more thorns, beginning to wonder if they were only going in circles.

Leaves rustled behind them, and then she heard heavy breathing. Not only were they lost, but Chester had managed to find them again.

Macy put more energy into her run. When they got a fork in the path, she tried to remember which direction they came from, but everything looked the same. Luke tugged on her arm, going right.

They came to another fork and turned left. After about only five steps, she slammed into someone—it had to be Chester. Macy looked up and saw him, the moonlight gleaming against his lenses.

He reached out and grabbed her. "Finally, I got you, Heather. It's time to go home and discuss your punishment. For your sake, I hope the prophets don't want to get involved. I'll go a lot easier on you than them."

Macy squirmed, kicking at him. "Yeah, I bet you will."

Chester dug his fingers into her arms. "You know I will."

She turned her head and bit into his wrist as hard as she could. She could taste blood, but she continued to bite down even harder.

"Let go of her." Luke punched Chester across the face.

He ripped his arm from her mouth and then lunged for Luke, who moved out of the way causing Chester to land on the ground with a thud.

Macy spit the blood out, wiping it on her white shirt.

Luke grabbed onto her arm and she ran, stumbling over her feet. She caught herself before falling and ran as fast as she could. But she only got a couple yards before she felt a tugging on her shirt, which made her gag.

Chester pulled her so close she could smell the strong community soap on him. "Stop fighting me. I lost you once, and that's not going to happen again—ever." He pulled on the shirt again, choking her. She pushed against him, kicking. She was aiming for his crotch, but couldn't reach at the angle he held her.

Luke ran at them, but Chester pulled a gun out with his free hand and shoved it in Luke's face.

"No!" Macy begged.

She twisted her body and forced herself down at an angle that forced him to loosen his grip. She gasped for air and ran. Luke grabbed her arm and they ran together.

Chester was barely a few steps behind. He kept reaching for her. She could feel his fingers rub against her back, unable to grab onto her shirt.

Macy picked up her speed, ignoring the pain in her lungs. She still hadn't gotten her breath fully back after his choking her. She gasped for air, not really able to get any decent breaths.

The path ended right in front of her, so she couldn't turn anywhere. Not having time to process that, she slammed into a tree. Chester pinned her against it, wrapping his arms around her.

He forced the gun into her temple.

"Get out of here, Luke, or I'll kill her."

"You wouldn't."

"Would you like to find out?" Chester asked. Something on the gun clicked.

Macy let out a cry.

"Macy, I can't leave you," Luke said.

"Go," Macy begged. "Save yourself."

"No, save her," Chester said. "Get out of here or you'll be wearing her brains, kid."

"Find a way out and finish our plan," Macy said.

Chester moved the gun toward Luke. "I changed my mind. There's no reason for me to let you go."

"Don't!" screamed Macy. "Run, Luke. Please."

"Oh, aren't you two cute?" Chester asked. He shoved the gun against Macy's temple. "You'd better leave now, Luke. My finger's about to slip."

Fear covered Luke's face. "I'll be back for you." Luke held her eye contact for a moment and then ran out of sight.

Macy couldn't move her arms or upper body. She couldn't even reach down to bite him again. However, she could still kick, so that's what she did. She kicked him as hard as she could, screaming at the top of her lungs.

"Do you really think that's going to help anything, Heather? Like I said, you should hope the prophets don't get involved with your punishment."

Macy squirmed and twisted, barely able to move. She twisted and swayed, finally getting a little room. She elbowed him in the stomach, and he let out a gasp, momentarily loosening his grip. Macy ran away from him, but when she looked back, he was already running after her.

Turning her head back around, she picked up her speed. As soon as she felt a tug on her shirt again, she ran faster, but his grip made her stumble, and she found herself falling straight for the ground. She put her hands out to protect her face from the impending dirt.

Dirt flew into Macy's eyes as her face hit the ground. Chester landed next to her with a thud. She wiped at her eyes frantically, the dirt burning them.

Chester wrapped his arms around her so tightly she could barely breathe. She struggled against him while still trying to get the painful flecks out of her eyes. Unable to see, she shoved her hands in his face, hoping to throw off his glasses again.

"It's not much fun when you can't see, is it? Funny how fast karma acts at times."

Macy threw her weight against him, kicking and clawing at him, hating him all the more for that comment. Somehow the last piece of dirt finally flew from her eye, but she still couldn't see because her eyes watered so much.

"Oh, did I make you cry? Or do you actually have remorse for running away?"

"No!" She fought back harder, but he just laughed and then somehow managed to stand up and pull her up, too.

"It's over, Heather. You need to give up."

"I'm not Heather." She kicked, hit, and squirmed more. Her feet weren't touching the ground, making it all the more difficult.

"We're back to *that* again, are we? You know you're Heather. I don't know why you keep fighting me. You must have learned disobedience from your first mom." He stopped and stared into her eyes. "Do you want to know what that got her? She's dead. Heather, your mom isn't in Paris, living the high life with some guy named Jacques. That's what happens to people who refuse to obey me. Don't think you're immune, either. You'd do well to learn from your true mom."

"I knew it! I knew you killed Karla, too." She kneed him in the crotch and he let out a yell, loosening his grip.

Macy stumbled as her feet hit the ground. Anger flashed over his face, but she ran away from him while she had the chance. Her only hope was finding her way to Luke and then getting out of the woods.

Macy took a few turns, pretty sure that she was going the way she came, but it was hard to tell with the paths being worse than a maze. She went a while without running into any intersecting paths. Finally, she ran into another wall of trees, too thick to get through. She stopped, gasping for air and listening for Chester.

If she couldn't get away from Chester, would this be it for her? Was it really over?

Macy heard running. She froze. Where was Chester? She walked down the path until she reached another one and then she looked around. Chester was nowhere to be seen. She could still hear fast footsteps somewhere close, but she couldn't see anything. Macy knew she had to keep moving. If she didn't, he would definitely find her again.

Still breathing deeply, she walked down the path. She could still hear the running, but it sounded far enough away that she was safe, at least for the time being. She couldn't get out of the forest on her own. Hopefully Luke was close by.

The footsteps sounded closer. Did they belong to Luke or Chester? Macy stopped again. She couldn't even tell where they came from. She held her breath.

She couldn't hear anymore running. It was her only chance. Macy burst into a run, not giving herself the chance to over-think anything. Maybe her instincts would take her where she needed to go. She ran, not seeing anyone.

As she passed two intersecting paths, she saw Chester from the corner of her eyes. Her stomach twisted in knots, but before she even had the chance to pick up speed, he leaped toward her and grabbed at her again. She could feel his fingers brush against her side, but he didn't get her or her shirt.

Macy ran faster, but tripped over something. Stumbling, she regained her balance, but she could sense Chester behind her. He wasn't going to give up. She felt his fingers again. Then a tugging on her shirt. He had managed to grasp it again. Macy picked up speed, feeling the resistance.

She had layers. Let him rip the shirt off. At an intersection, she turned without warning. Macy could still feel his hold as she took another sharp turn.

Chester yanked on her shirt. Macy pulled the other way and somehow ended up landing on the ground again. She closed her eyes, not getting anything in them. She could feel the ground scrape against her face as she slid, stopping only inches from a large boulder.

He landed on top of Macy, knocking the wind out of her. He grabbed a chunk of her hair and yanked her head back. "You need to make a choice, and you need to make it now. Stop fighting me. It's your only choice, really. Unless you actually want to join Dorcas and your first mom."

Macy couldn't answer. She still couldn't get a decent breath. She felt the gun pressed against her head again.

"Silence is not an option, Heather. Either you're on my side or not."

Macy refused to speak. He couldn't make her.

"Do you need some convincing, Heather?"

Macy didn't say anything. She heard a horrible popping sound and then felt a searing pain in her leg.

"Want me to break the other one?" He moved off her.

This was her last chance. She got up and ran, but as soon as her sore leg hit the ground, she felt an even worse pain. Macy lost her balance and fell into a patch of pricker bushes.

Dark

MACY OPENED HER eyes, but still didn't see anything because of the darkness. She felt around. Softness surrounded her. She had to have been in a bed.

She couldn't still be in the community. It didn't feel like that hard, uncomfortable bed. That one had been stiff and the bedding smelled like that awful soap they used for everything. She pulled a blanket up to her face. It had a light, pleasant scent. She didn't recognize it, so she couldn't be back at the farm house or in her own bed, either.

Where *was* she?

Macy tried to move her legs, but only one would comply.

A fire came to mind, and then the escaping in the woods only to be found by Chester again. She couldn't remember anything after that. Had Chester caught her?

Macy looked around the room, hoping that her eyes would have adjusted, but she still couldn't see a thing. She sat up. She hadn't gone blind, had she?

She felt her eyes and they were fine. Macy breathed a sigh of relief. She felt her left leg. Something hard covered it. It had to have been a cast. Had she been in a hospital? She couldn't be in one, because she knew they never kept rooms pitch black.

Leaning back down, Macy decided not to worry about it. She appeared to be safe, at least for the time being. The bed smelled clean and was comfortable. Even more important, Chester didn't appear to be nearby.

Feeling sleepy, she closed her eyes. She thought of Luke. Had he been able to get out of the forest? He wouldn't have returned to the community, would he?

She felt tears gearing up. Why had she insisted on leaving the community that night? Dorcas would still be alive, and she would at least have been able to see Luke at school. And what had happened to the kids at campsite?

The light came on, assaulting her eyes. Macy covered them with her arm. She heard someone moving around in the room. Did they know she had woken?

Macy moved her arm away from her eyes, but the light was still too bright. She blinked several times. The light finally felt normal so she looked around.

Rebekah stood folding clothes with her back to Macy.

"Where am I?" Macy asked.

Rebekah turned around. She wore plain but colored clothes and had her hair down, making her look even prettier than she had with the white garb.

"Your dad said you might not recognize it here since it had been so long. This is your old room, Heather."

Macy looked around. They weren't at the farm house. It had to be the house that Heather had been in when her mom had gone missing. Could this be the room where she had written her diaries before being taken to a mental hospital?

She looked around at the furniture. The dresser was the one that had been in her room in the farm house. She had found one of Heather's diaries in there. Macy recognized the shelf full of books and DVDs where she had found another diary.

"What's going on?" she asked.

"I'm folding your clothes. You're supposed to rest." Rebekah sounded mad.

"Is my leg broken?"

Rebekah continued with the clothes. "I wouldn't know. We wrapped it up, but aren't taking you to the hospital. It'll have to heal on its own, whatever's wrong with it. Your knee swelled badly, so my guess is that it's sprained."

"Why are we here?"

She turned and stared at Macy. "Because of what you did."

"What?"

Anger covered her face. "I did everything I could to help you feel at home in the community. I even kept your friendship with Luke a secret, but I never would have if I had known what you two were plotting."

"Why aren't we back there?"

"Why? Because we got kicked out. All of us. Because of you."

"Even you? Couldn't you have—?"

"No, I couldn't. Marriage is forever. Where my husband goes, I follow. So, here we are. Back in the world. But you're staying in the house for a while. Even if you weren't stuck here because of that leg, he said you're to stay in the house. You're not going anywhere for a long time, Heather."

Disagree

CHAD PUBLISHED HIS latest post, this one a regular sports post. As much as it had killed him, a couple weeks before, he had to stop the daily postings about Macy. There were only so many ways he could spin the same thing, and it had been weeks since there was anything new to report. Not only that, but his page views were going down, which meant that people had either lost interest or given up on ever finding her.

He wasn't going to give up on her, but at the same time, he had to find a way to move on with his life until she returned. And part of that meant taking care of the rest of the family. Alyssa had become more distraught as time went by. It was nearly spring, and Macy had been gone since before Thanksgiving.

Chad checked for new comments and responded right away. His heart wasn't in it, but he wrote with his typical humor on the sports posts. The comments on his Macy posts had moved from sad condolences to theories and people sharing what clues they thought they had found. His response to the clues was telling people to contact the cops if they thought it was real.

Chad picked up his phone, looking for any missed calls or texts. Detective Fleshman was supposed to get back to him that morning. They still didn't have any results from the DNA of the young Jane Doe in the morgue. The first set had been compromised somehow and the next batch had come up inconclusive. Chad certainly didn't understand the medical mumbo-jumbo he and Alyssa had been told. All he knew was that they didn't have the answers they desperately needed.

Would they ever have the results? The body had to be decomposing, even though they probably had ways to slow the process.

The screen in front of him was blurry. It was time for a break. He got up and stretched before going upstairs.

Alex and Zoey sat at the kitchen table with text books, papers, and laptops spread all over the table.

"How's the studying?"

Alex scowled. "I hate history. How is it relevant? Math at least makes sense."

Chad patted Alex's head. "They say those who don't learn history are doomed to repeat it."

"Whatever." Alex went back to his work.

Zoey looked up. "Any word from the police?"

"Not yet."

Her face fell. "When are we going to know?"

Chad pulled some leftovers out from the fridge. "Wish I knew." He scooped some food onto a plate and put it in the microwave. "I keep checking my phone. They have to get some results this time. The third time's a charm, right?"

"I hope so. Or we'll have to wait even longer."

Alex got up and grabbed a pop. "Maybe by then she'll be back home and it won't matter. We all know that dead chick isn't Macy."

"We *hope* it's not her," Zoey said.

"It's not." Alex sat down, twisted the cap off and drank.

Zoey rubbed her stomach, looking sad.

Chad tried not to think about what was under her over-sized shirt—his grandchild. He was barely past forty and he had to think about being a grandparent. It was crazy, but nothing was harder to believe than his thirteen year old becoming a dad. He still couldn't wrap his mind around that one.

"When do your parents get in, Zoey?" asked Chad.

She made a face. "Don't remind me. I wish she'd just stay in Japan with him. Maybe they'll get into a big fight and he'll decide not to come here. Why do you ask? You trying to get rid of me?"

"What?" Chad asked. "No. You're always welcome here. Just like always." Why did he feel like he was digging himself into a hole? "Do you want anything while I'm up?"

"No, but thanks." Zoey went back to her studies. They were both doing an online homeschooling program because they couldn't deal with the social pressures and everything else.

The microwave beeped and Chad got his food and then escaped to the bonus room. He turned on the TV and the news came on. After about fifteen minutes, he realized that they hadn't once mentioned Macy. That made him almost as upset as when they wouldn't stop talking about her. He wasn't sure which was worse.

Alyssa walked by the doorway and then doubled back and sat down next to him. "Did you hear from Fleshman yet?"

He shook his head, his mouth full of beans.

"Me neither." Her lips curled down. "I wish they would at least tell us something. I hate waiting. It seems like that's all we do anymore."

Chad swallowed. "It's not their fault. The tests are being done in Seattle. Maybe even being sent out? The whole thing is confusing, and I can't keep it straight."

"It has to be her."

He nearly choked on broccoli. "What?"

"She's been missing for almost four months, Chad. There haven't been any new clues since, what, December?"

"So you think Macy's dead?"

Tears filled her eyes. "What else am I supposed to think?"

"That she's alive! We can't give up on her." He set his plate down on the coffee table a little too hard.

"What does it matter? We can't do anything about it. Whether she's alive or dead, she's not with us. I, for one, need to mourn. Living in limbo is killing me."

"Then we need to get out and form another search party. If we start one, there are plenty of people who will join us. I can print off more fliers."

"It's not going to *do* anything. Everyone around here already knows that she's missing. Her pictures have been plastered everywhere for months. I need closure."

"Closure? Are you serious?"

Alyssa narrowed her eyes. "Do I look like I'm kidding?"

"You can move on with your life without having closure. You don't need to believe that our daughter is dead. Get back to going to the gym— not that you need to, you look great. Join the book club again. You used to really enjoy that. But don't give up on Macy. Please."

Alyssa's eyes shone with tears. "We have to face reality, Chad. With every day that goes by, and there have been a lot of days, the chances go down of her coming home safely."

Chad took a deep breath. He needed to tread carefully or they would find themselves arguing again, like they had before Macy disappeared. The last thing he wanted was to lose what they'd gained.

He put his arm around Alyssa. "Whatever you do, I'm behind you."

"But you think I'm an idiot for thinking she's dead. I can see it in your eyes. You're living in a Pollyanna world, believing that everything will end up working out. How can it? One baby is gone and the other is going have a baby of his own."

Counting to ten silently, Chad took deep breaths. He spoke slowly. "I like to believe that I'm living in a place of reality, but we can agree to disagree on that. As far as the baby, we don't even know if Zoey is going to keep it."

"Seriously? She's going to make up her mind after holding the baby. There's no way she's going to give up her baby after *holding* it. She's going to fall in love immediately. That's how it works."

"Or she could take one look at the little face and realize she's not ready for the responsibility. She could love the baby enough to make the right decision to give it to a family who desperately wants one."

Alyssa shook her head. "You really do live in a fantasy world."

"Look, I'm trying my best to be patient, but if you keep saying things like that, I can't give you any guarantees. Let's agree to disagree. If we have to, we'll avoid the topic."

"Agree to disagree? We're not talking about wallpaper, Chad. These discussions can't be avoided."

Chad took another slow, deliberate breath. "All I'm saying is that we love each other. The world is falling apart around us and we need to stick together. Macy isn't here, and there's not a damn thing we can do about it. We've done everything we can, and now we just have to live with her absence. Our thirteen year old is going to make us grandparents and we can't change that, either. But we *can* hold onto each other."

She blinked and tears fell onto her face. "I wish I could believe that."

"What do you mean?"

"It's not that easy. Love isn't enough."

"I never said it would be easy. I said we need to stick together. For each other and our kids—regardless of how things end up." Chad begged her with his eyes. He needed her to keep hoping.

Alyssa took his hand. "I do love you. You and Alex are all I have."

"And Macy."

"Not any more." More tears fell.

Chad wanted to convince her that Macy was out there—that she needed them to not give up—but he knew it wouldn't get them anywhere. How could she give up? He scooted closer to her and wrapped his arms around her.

They sat in silence.

How would Chad get through this if she gave up?

After a while, he asked, "What's going on with Zoey?"

"What do you mean?"

"I asked her about her parents, and she got really upset."

"Don't you pay attention? She's hurt because her dad has never had any interest in being in her life. Now that she's pregnant and his career is over, he wants to be involved. Not only is it a slap in the face, but she has all those extra hormones to deal with. It's a double whammy. Teenage hormones and pregnancy. I can't imagine dealing with both at the same time."

"Oh, that explains it." He would never understand female hormones, but from what he had seen, they were very real. He remembered with Alyssa's pregnancies, he had to tread lightly. He would have to do double duty with Zoey.

Chad looked at his empty plate.

"Do you want me to make you something to eat and bring it up?"

"No. I can't eat. We need to start looking into funeral arrangements."

The room shrunk around him. "What?"

"She deserves a memorial service."

"Macy hasn't been pronounced dead. Can't you at least wait for that before you jump the gun?"

"You think I'm acting rash?"

"We haven't even gotten the DNA results back. We have no reason to believe the body is Macy. You can't do this. If she is alive somewhere, you'll just send her the message that we've given up."

"How can I get through to you, Chad? I need closure. I have to be able to say goodbye and move on with my life so I can focus on Alex. That poor kid needs us, and he's dealing with her loss, too. It's not fair. He deserves to have me taking care of him properly."

"He's actually doing pretty well if you hadn't noticed. His grades are higher than they've ever been. The teacher in charge of the online school says he may actually get through the eighth grade stuff before school gets out for the summer. He's not only caught up, but will probably get ahead."

Alyssa folded her arms. "He still needs me to be there for him fully. Not like I've been."

"You can do that without giving Macy a funeral, Lyss. We can act like a family again while still waiting for her to return."

"No, actually I can't. I'm not waiting for the mail, Chad. This is our daughter. I can't wait for her *and* continue on with my life. All I can think about is how she should be with us, but she's not."

They stared each other down. It was obvious that neither one was going to back down.

Arguing

CHAD CLOSED HIS laptop, his eyes heavy from responding to over a hundred comments. It had to be past midnight, but he didn't care to check the time. His stomach growled because he hadn't eaten since lunch. He didn't want to after that disagreement with Alyssa. How could she be so eager to plan Macy's funeral?

It didn't make sense to him, and he wasn't going to allow it. Macy wasn't dead, and he wasn't going let her have a funeral unless she was.

Why was Alyssa being so emotional—jumping to conclusions like this? She needed to keep a calm head. They all did. It was the only way they would make it through the ordeal until Macy did return.

Chad made his way up the stairs. The doors to both Macy's and Alex's rooms were closed with no light coming from underneath. Hopefully that meant Zoey and Alex were both sleeping in separate rooms, with Zoey staying in Macy's. Not that it mattered at that point where they slept.

The light was on in his and Alyssa's room, not that it surprised him. Alyssa was still sleeping at odd times. Sometimes she was too upset to sleep, other times, not being able to stay awake when she wanted to.

Chad stopped cold when he walked in. She had suitcases on their bed—his suitcases.

He steadied his voice. "What's going on, Lyss?"

"You need to move out for a little while."

"Excuse me?"

"We can't keep going on like this anymore."

"Like what?" he demanded.

"My point exactly."

"What's that supposed to mean?"

36

"You don't get it."

Anger ran through him. "There's nothing to *get*, Alyssa. Our daughter is missing and we don't agree on where she's at."

"Exactly. That's a major obstacle, and not one I'm willing to live with."

"So, basically you're going to threaten me with moving out if I don't agree with you? Nice. Really nice."

She narrowed her eyes. "It's not about choosing sides. It's about facing reality—and you refuse to do that. You're going to hang onto this forever. I can see it, twenty years from now, me begging to give our little girl a funeral and you putting your foot down, saying no, she's going to come back. Just wait. It's the beginning of March, Chad. I've done nothing but wait since the middle of November. When those test results finally come, you'll see who's right."

"Then wait for them to come in. Want me to call Fleshman right now? I can, and I'll probably wake him. You know what he'll tell us? He doesn't know. Don't you think if that body was Macy's, someone would be able to figure it out by now?"

"I bet if they would have let us look at it, we could have told them months ago," Alyssa said. "We could have moved on a long time ago."

"They don't want us dealing with the emotional trauma if it is her. The body is so messed up they couldn't identify her face or any markings."

"Yeah, and it has enough similarities to give reasonable doubt. Similar height, weight, and hair color. For whatever reason, they can't get those test results right. Why is that?" She stared him down.

"I don't know, but you need to put my clothes back on the hangers. I don't want them getting wrinkled."

"Hang them yourself when you get wherever you're going." Alyssa narrowed her eyes.

Chad went over to the bed and dumped out the closest luggage and then tossed the suitcase on the floor. "I'm not going anywhere."

"You're not staying here."

"Look. If you need space, that's fine. I'll sleep in the bonus room or even down in my office, but you're not kicking me out of my house. I've done nothing wrong."

"Not good enough." Alyssa folded her arms.

"You're right. I should have a bed. I'll take Macy's, because that's probably empty."

Alyssa glared at him. "I made sure they went to bed in the proper rooms."

"And I'm sure they stayed there, too," Chad said sarcastically. He dumped out the other suitcase. "Put those back on their hangers or I'm sending them all to the dry cleaner to get pressed. I'm not going to wear wrinkled clothes."

"Then don't dump them on the bed. I had them all nicely folded."

"Put them in the closet, then."

"Chad, I'm done arguing about your clothes. In fact, I'm done arguing, period."

"Good. Put my stuff away while I get ready for bed. You're going to have to deal with me snoring next to you, because I'm not going anywhere."

"Yes, you are."

He stepped closer to her. "I'm not going anywhere. I was willing to sleep in a different room, but now I'm not."

"You have to. I'm kicking you out."

Chad laughed bitterly. "Really? Out of my own house? The house that I paid for? Tell me, how are you going to pay for everything? Not just the house payment, but the utilities. Everything costs money, and you don't make anything. Not that you couldn't. You could make more than I could. But you don't. You like being a domestic engineer and I'm happy to provide that for you. But not if you try kicking me out of the house I've worked so hard for."

Her lips formed a straight line and her face reddened. "Have you heard of child support and alimony?"

"Don't threaten it unless you mean it. Do you hear me? Don't even go there unless you're prepared. And just to let you know, the state of Washington doesn't do alimony. You could get child support, but not spousal. And believe me, since I'm the one with the money, I could afford a much better attorney than you. Like I said, don't go there unless you're serious."

She looked shaken. Good. How dare she throw this at him? Attempting to kick him out and then throw divorce at him. What had gotten into her?

"How do you know so much about that?" she asked.

"I haven't looked into it, if that's what you're implying. Half the people we know are split. Men gossip in the office too, you know. So, have you changed your mind?"

"You won't go?" she asked.

"I think I've made myself clear. If you need to get away from me, take some time and visit your parents. I'll even pay for a first class plane ticket. Even when you're threatening me with divorce and alimony."

"You think going to my parents' house is going to help?"

Maybe they could talk some sense into her. "It would get you away from me, and since you obviously don't want to be anywhere near me it might help."

"Chad, this isn't a joke."

"I'm not kidding around, Lyss."

"Well, if we're going to make this work, we have to get on the same page," she said.

"Then we either have to agree to disagree or you're going to have to agree to wait for actual proof before planning a memorial service. And let me tell you something. Even if you leave me and keep planning it, I'm going to fight you every step of the way. No one should have a funeral unless they're actually dead. I won't let that happen to Macy."

She stepped closer to him. "And when someone is dead, they deserve a memorial."

"We have no proof. Wait until the results come in. Then we'll know who's right and what to do."

"Or we'll just find out that particular girl isn't her. Then we'll be back to knowing nothing. We may never find a body. Then what?"

"Why are you doing this? How can you give up?"

"Give up? You think I'm giving up?"

"What else would you call it?"

"You're impossible. Really, you won't just leave?"

"I'm not going anywhere."

"Only me."

"Only you what?"

"Anyone else kicks their husband out and they go. Not me."

"You know what I think? I think a good night's rest is in order. It's late and we're tired. Let's talk about this in the morning."

"If you won't go, then I will."

"Where are you going? Flights are much more expensive when you purchase them at the airport."

Alyssa's face flushed red. "My parents aren't the only people I know. Do you think I'm that much of a loser?"

"Of course not. Are you going to stay at a friend's house? How long?"

"I'm not your child! I don't have to tell you what I'm doing. In fact, I don't have to tell you anything."

Sadness ran through Chad, replacing the anger. "Are you sure you want to go, Lyss? Really, I'll sleep in another room and we can talk about this again in the morning. Or we can talk tomorrow night. I'll give you all the space you need."

She gave him an exasperated look. "You really don't get it."

"Clearly."

They stared at each other. Chad tried to express with his eyes where his mouth had failed. They needed each other more than ever. Separating, even for a short time, wasn't going to make anything better.

Finally he said, "I hope you won't go."

"Since you won't, you leave me no choice."

"Please, Alyssa. Think about all the tough times we've gone through. Being together is what helped us. We need each other now more than ever. You say you want to be here for Alex—do you really think that taking off is going to help him? His sister is missing and—"

"You don't need to explain what's going on in my son's life. He's old enough and smart enough to know this isn't about him."

"Let me brush my teeth and then you can have the bedroom." Chad let out a slow breath as he walked to their bathroom. Tears were threatening, but he had to hold it together. What had gotten into her? Was it the grief talking? Did she have her own hormonal issues? She was too young for the female life change, wasn't she?

He took his time brushing and going to the bathroom, hoping that a strike of brilliance would hit him. That way when he came out of the bathroom, he could say the right thing and she would change her mind so they could fall asleep in each other's arms.

By the time he was done, he had no such strike of luck. He looked around the empty bedroom. Had she gone to check on the kids? He went down the hall, finding it empty. He went through the rest of the house, still not finding her.

Heart sinking, he looked outside to where her car had been for the last couple of days.

It wasn't there. Knowing it wouldn't be in the garage, he looked anyway. His car sat there, looking lonely and dejected.

Or was that Chad?

Sorrows

ALYSSA PULLED INTO the same parking spot she had the last time she was at the bar. Drinking hadn't solved any problems then, but at least she had been able to forget her troubles for a little while. She looked around the parking lot, relieved to see Rusty's tow truck missing.

The last thing she needed was a lecture from him again. She wasn't going to drink and drive, so there was nothing to feel guilty about. She had packed a pillow and blankets so she would sleep in the back of her car. If Rusty did show up, insisting to tow her again, this time she had cash to pay him and for the hotel he would drop her off at.

She fixed her hat, making sure it covered her eyes. Her family was practically at celebrity status between being on the news for Macy's disappearance and Chad's blog. Over the last month, he had had them making videos and uploading them to the blog since the news hadn't been talking about the case as much.

Her face was everywhere and the last thing she wanted was to be recognized. She only wanted to drink as many fishbowls of alcohol as she could without passing out. Not that losing consciousness sounded so bad. Anything to take her away from her life and the constant reminders of what a failure she was. One kid missing and the other ready to become a parent. They would certainly skip over her when handing out the Mother of Year award.

Walking into the bar, she was glad to see it was busy. No one paid any attention to her.

There was only one available table way in the back. She couldn't have asked for anything more. She sat down and watched everyone while she waited for the waitress. There were several lively games of pool going on as well as plenty of TVs with different sports to choose from. There were also quite a few loud conversations, with people who had already had too much to drink. It was no wonder that Rusty came to this bar. He probably made a fine living towing drunks home.

The same waitress from months earlier made her way to Alyssa's table, again chewing a big wad of gum. She listed off the specials for the night, holding a pad of paper and a pen. Alyssa noticed her name tag said Sela.

"Do you still have the fishbowl drinks?"

"Yeah, but they're not on special. Have you tried—?"

"I'll take a fishbowl. I don't care what it costs."

"Fishbowl it is." She wrote on the paper. "Anything else?"

Alyssa remembered the nachos not going over so well. "Surprise me with your favorite appetizer."

The waitress smiled and nodding, writing. "Sure thing." She walked away.

Yawning, Alyssa hoped the food and drink would help to wake her up. It was late and she hadn't slept well since Macy disappeared. Hopefully tonight she could forget all about everything and finally get the sleep she needed. She watched the nearest game of pool, trying to convince herself it was interesting.

Sela brought over a fishbowl and set it on the table. "The food's still cooking."

"Thanks, Sela." She grabbed the straw and drank as fast as she could. Feeling warm, Alyssa took her coat off. She wanted to take the itchy hat off, but she didn't want anyone to recognize her. Especially Rusty. Maybe she would be lucky and he was driving drunks home from a different bar that night.

Just as she emptied the fishbowl, Sela came with a steaming plate. From Alyssa's angle, she couldn't see what was on it.

Sela's eyes widened. "Ready for another bowl already?"

Alyssa pushed it toward her, nodding.

"I'll get that for you right away." She set the food in front of Alyssa. It looked like a combo platter. It had cheese sticks, onion rings, tiny baked potatoes, egg rolls, quesadilla slices, and little chicken wings. It was enough for two or three, but Alyssa didn't care. Her mouth watered as she tried to decide what to eat first.

She looked up to say thank you, but Sela had already disappeared. Alyssa picked up an egg roll and bit down. It melted in her mouth. It was even better than the food at her favorite Chinese restaurant.

When she had a mouth full of a baked potato, Sela arrived with another fishbowl. Not wanting to be rude by not thanking her twice in a row, Alyssa gave her thumbs-up.

"No problem. Enjoy."

Alyssa planned to. She finished the potato and then went to work on the new fishbowl. Before long, she was eating, but not even aware of what was in her mouth. She had finished most of the platter, having left all of the cheese sticks. She was used to the kids eating all of those, so it was just habit.

"You again."

Looking up, Alyssa saw Rusty standing next to her. It took a moment to register because of her buzz. She wanted to groan, knowing a lecture was coming, but he was so gorgeous she couldn't. The way his curls fell around his face and ears was too much. "Hi, Rusty."

"Mind if I sit down?"

"Sure. Have some food. It's the least I can do since you paid my bill last time."

"Don't forget about the free ride home." He smiled.

Oh, heavens, that smile. What was he doing as tow truck driver? Alyssa knew she should have been embarrassed, but she couldn't take her eyes off his face.

Rusty picked up a cheese stick and took a bite. "I've always loved these. I haven't seen you around in a while. I had hoped you were doing okay."

He had thought about her? Alyssa started to smile, but then remembered her face was everywhere. How could he have not thought about her? She shrugged, not wanting to talk about her life. She had gone there to forget. Or had she actually wanted to see Rusty? There *were* plenty of bars between her house and this one.

It was hard to remember why she had come here, although she was more than aware of her fight with Chad. That jerk wouldn't leave the house like a normal husband.

"What brings you here?" Rusty picked up another cheese stick.

"Nothing I want to talk about."

He nodded. "What do you want to talk about?"

She looked at the platter. "These onion rings. Have you ever tasted anything like them? It's like food from heaven."

Rusty laughed, the skin around his eyes crinkling. He looked even more beautiful. "They are pretty good." He looked at the fishbowl. "How many have you had?"

"Only two."

"Looks like you'll need another ride home then."

"Oh, seriously."

He shook his head, his curls bouncing around.

She waved Sela over. "I'll take another fishbowl."

"Coming right up." She eyed Rusty and walked off, not giving him a chance to say no.

"You really think you need a third one?"

"I came here to forget about life. So, yeah, I do need another."

"Haven't you forgotten yet?"

Alyssa shook her head. "I only have a buzz. I need to get plastered."

"Plastered, huh? Well, I'd better stay here with you then. You mind the company?"

"Not at all. I could look at you all night." She could feel her face turn bright red. Why had she said that?

Rusty's face looked a little pink as well. "Okay, I suppose that works. You'll let me tow you home?"

"I'm just going to sleep in my car. You can tow someone else to-night."

"You're planning to spend the night in your car—in this neighbor-hood? Have you lost your mind?"

"That's pretty much why I came here. To lose it. You know what I mean. To forget everything. Now I'm not even making sense to myself."

"I can't let you sleep in your car."

"I told you I'm not going home."

He nodded and then took the last onion ring. "Manna from heaven."

Was he trying to distract her? She nodded, faking a smile. "You can drop me off at a hotel. Anywhere but home."

"We don't have to talk about it. What shows do you like to watch?"

Alyssa stopped. "I can't remember the last time I watched something."

"What did you used to watch?"

Sela dropped off the fishbowl and Rusty looked at her. "We'll get the check now. No more drinks."

"Sure thing, Rusty."

Why did Alyssa feel so bad at the mention of shows? Probably because it reminded her of the fact that she hadn't done anything normal in such a long time. Maybe that was part of the reason she felt like getting out of the house—that and the fact that Chad refused to leave.

She grabbed the bowl and took the longest sip she could manage. Alyssa didn't want to think about home or Chad or anything. Swallowing, she looked at Rusty, feeling a bit dizzy. "So what have you been up to?"

"Same old. Towing people home to keep them off the streets."

"Is that all you do? And you do it for free?"

"Not usually. A man does have to make a living." He grinned. Like a Greek god.

"Have you considered modeling?" Alyssa asked.

Rusty raised an eyebrow. "Modeling? No."

"You could rake in a lot more with that than driving a tow truck. You could always do that for your good deed of the day."

He shook his head, the beautiful curls jumping around again. "No interest in modeling." How was he still single?

Alyssa had never looked at another man other than Chad in all their years together, but there was something she really liked about Rusty. Her mind wasn't working clearly enough to figure out why.

She took another drink.

"Are you done with that?"

"It's half full."

"I'll pay for it if you stop now."

Alyssa held up her purse. "I brought plenty of money. I don't need a handout."

"Think of it as me paying you to stop."

"You already know I'm not climbing into my car. Not to drive it, anyway."

"And you're aware that you're going to ride in my truck while I tow your car. I don't want you spreading the manna all over my interior." Did his eyes twinkle, or was that her imagination?

She smiled. "My stomach feels fine."

Sela came by with the bill and Rusty took it.

Alyssa snatched it from him. "I told you I have the money."

He tapped the table. "If you leave the drink alone, you can pay. Otherwise, I will."

She raised an eyebrow. "Are you for real?"

"That's the deal."

Men. Why were they always trying to control her? First with Chad refusing to leave and now this. "Fine." She shoved the bowl as far away from her as possible. "Happy?"

"Satisfied."

Alyssa grabbed her purse and found the pocket with the cash. She pulled out enough for everything plus a tip and then set it on top of the receipt.

"You ready to go?" Rusty ran his hands through his hair, leaning back.

"Not really. Why don't we sit here and wait for the alcohol to make its way through me. Then you can leave without having to worry about the free tow."

"It's not really free. I write it off at tax time. I actually have an appointment with my accountant, so I could use another write-off."

"You know what I mean."

"This place is going to close before you're ready to drive safely."

"I told you I'm not driving."

"And I'm not letting you sleep in this neighborhood."

They stared at each other.

"You're impossible." Alyssa shook her head. Maybe it was a man thing.

Rusty leaned forward, raising an eyebrow. "Actually, you are."

"Me? You've lost your mind."

"Nope. It's perfectly sound." He grinned.

"What are we going to do? Tow me to a hotel?" She shrugged. "Or I could just sleep here."

"In the bar?"

"Yeah. Why not?"

"For starters, they don't allow it. Then we're back to the fact that I won't leave you in this neighborhood in your car."

"I hope you're able to come up with a good suggestion, because I'm done. I'm perfectly happy sleeping in the car."

Rusty sighed, looking worn out or perhaps frustrated. He was quiet for a minute before speaking again. "I have a spare room at my house. We actually used it as a guest room, but I haven't had anyone over since the accident."

She stared at him. "You want me to go back to your place?"

"It's not like that. I don't want to drop you off at a hotel. I'd feel a lot better if someone was there to watch out for you."

"I'm not a kid."

"No, you're not. But I want to make sure you're okay. Last time, you went home to your family. This time, you're refusing. You can even lock the guest room, if you'd feel better about staying there. And it's at the other end of the house from my room. It's either that or I'm taking you home."

Alyssa frowned. "Do you do this for everyone?"

His lips curled into a smile. "Never."

Guest

ALYSSA TRIPPED WALKING into Rusty's house. It was a lot nicer than she had expected from a bachelor pad. He must have left everything the way his wife had and then hired a cleaning service, because no guy she knew was that tidy. The front room practically sparkled.

She looked around, taking it all in. It was a sprawling rambler on a large lot. Even though it was dark, and the house too big to see the back yard, she pictured a large play structure where the kids had probably spent hours playing.

That was probably why he had taken a special interest in her. They had both lost children and that was something that most people couldn't understand. Alyssa sure wished that she didn't. Even with fishbowls full of alcohol, she couldn't truly forget.

"You have a really nice place."

Rusty closed and locked the front door. "Thanks. I left it the way Lani left it. She had a real eye for design."

Alyssa nodded, afraid the alcohol would make her say something stupid. For the first time since ordering, she regretted drinking so much. She didn't trust her mouth, but felt like she should say something nice about his wife. She just didn't dare yet.

"Are you tired? I can show you to the guest room or I can show you around. What do you feel like?"

Her stomach squeezed. "Actually, could you show me to the bathroom?"

"Uh, oh. Follow me." He led her down a hall to the right and pointed to a door. "There you go."

She nodded a thanks and ran in, closing the door. Alyssa flipped on the light switch and the fan. Hopefully the fan was loud enough that he wouldn't hear her retching. She got to the toilet just in time.

Ordering food when drinking that much was a waste of time and money.

When she was finally done throwing up, she splashed water on her face and then found some toothpaste and put some on her finger. She rubbed it on her teeth and then swished it around her mouth.

After rinsing, she went into the hall and didn't see him. That was a relief. Even though he probably knew she was losing her food—again—at least he had given her privacy. She went down the hall from where she came and saw the front room was empty. Where had he gone? She didn't even know where she was supposed to crash.

"Rusty?"

Silence.

Alyssa's heart rate picked up. What was going on? Maybe coming to his house had been a bad idea. "Are you awake?"

A noise from the left startled her. Rusty appeared and gave her his gorgeous smile. "Sorry. I decided to use the restroom too. Do you want the grand tour before I show you to your room?"

Relief flooded her and she smiled back. "That sounds great." It was strange to be alone in a house with a guy other than Chad, but she felt perfectly at ease with Rusty.

"This way." He went back down the hall and she followed, unable to avoid noticing that he was just as easy on the eyes from the back as the front. She took her gaze off him and looked at the pictures on the wall. It was a shrine to his beautiful family.

They entered a large, bright kitchen. It was modern and gorgeous. For a moment, Alyssa was jealous, but then she remembered that he was probably quite lonely in such a large kitchen that must have held so many memories.

Rusty leaned against the island, nearly bumping his head on one of the pots hanging from the ceiling. "Feel free to use the kitchen whenever you wish. If you're hungry, eat. Use whatever looks good." He winked.

"Maybe I will. I owe you for the tows and now for giving me place to stay."

"You don't owe me anything. But if you do feel you need to repay me, please consider dropping the alcohol. I told you what I went through after losing my family. Rehab sucks."

Alyssa held onto her stomach. "No. That's okay. I'm already thinking about finding a new way to deal with my grief."

"You want some toast or crackers?"

She shook her head.

"You're looking pretty green, Mrs. Mercer."

"Alyssa. Please call me Alyssa."

"Of course. Would you prefer toast or crackers? Your stomach needs something bland." He indicated for her to sit at the table.

He wasn't going to take no for an answer, was he? "Crackers are fine." She sat down at the nearest chair.

Rusty went into the pantry and came out with a white box and opened it, pouring square crackers onto a plate. He set it in front of her and then sat across from her. "Do you need to call anyone and let them know you won't be home tonight?"

"I made that clear before I left." She picked up a cracker and bit into it, spilling crumbs onto the table. "Sorry."

"No problem. Anything you want to talk about? I'm all ears."

She looked into his beautiful eyes. He looked like he actually wanted to listen.

"People often tell me their troubles as I tow them places. I'm good at keeping secrets." He gave her a reassuring nod.

Alyssa let out a slow, deliberate sigh. Did she dare open up? Maybe she should wait to make that decision until after the alcohol had left her system. "I really appreciate you opening your home to me, Rusty, but I'm suddenly exhausted. I hope you're not offended if I just go to bed?"

"Not at all." He stood up. "Let me show you to your room. It's just down the hall."

Still feeling the buzz, Alyssa held onto the table as she got up from the chair. She followed him down another hall and ended up facing several doors.

Rusty pointed to one on the left. "That's another bathroom and the laundry room. And that one," he pointed to the door at the end of the hall, "leads to the back yard. The one behind you is the guest room. Do you need anything? You didn't bring in a bag."

Alyssa shook her head. "It's in my car."

"Want me to fetch it for you?"

"I can get it."

"No, I'm steadier on my feet. I'll only be a minute."

"Can't argue with that." She dug her keys out of her purse and handed him the one that went to her car.

He took off, and Alyssa used the bathroom again. She really shouldn't have drunk that much. There had to be another way to deal with her life. She had been sneaking more of Chad's beers—and she didn't even like beer. He had to have noticed, but hadn't said anything.

Sighing she flushed the toilet. After washing her hands, she looked around the room. It was as Rusty had described. A full bathroom with a washer and dryer and shelving that held laundry items. She grabbed a washcloth and ran it under warm water and washed her face. Too bad she hadn't brought her creams, but she hadn't thought that far ahead.

When she got into the hall, she didn't see Rusty. Maybe she should have told him where the bag was. Her car was an embarrassing mess. She hadn't been taking care of it since Macy disappeared. That was something else that needed to change along with giving up alcohol. She had to get her life back, even though it would never be close to the same again. Living in limbo was done.

Alyssa went into the room that Rusty had said would be hers for the night. She found the light switch and turned it on. The first thing she saw was her bag sitting in the middle of a queen sized bed. Her keys were on top of the bag.

She closed the door behind her and stuck her keys in the purse and then dug her pajamas out from the bag. Soon she was in the middle of the ultra-soft bed all by herself. When was the last time she had gone to bed and not had to worry about anyone disturbing her? If one of the kids didn't need her, then Chad did.

Guilt stabbed at her for enjoying the peace. She shoved it away. After everything she had done for everyone all those years, there was nothing wrong with taking some time to take care of herself. Even with all the stress and heartache of Macy being gone, she had still taken care of Alex, Chad, and even Zoey.

Not that she minded taking care of everyone. Even Chad, who could take care of himself. Sure, she had spent a lot of time sobbing by herself—especially in the beginning—but she had also made sure that everyone was taken care. She'd had to step it up when people stopped bringing over meals.

Alyssa had taken that as her first small sign that it was time to move on with life. Things needed to return to normal as much as possible. They were still alive, and she needed to get herself together enough to take care of her remaining child. Alex was who she had to focus on now. She needed this time to pull herself together without distraction.

Before she could focus on taking care of Alex properly, she needed to mourn Macy. She would allow herself to grieve while she had this bedroom all by herself, and then she would plan the funeral—even if it ruined her relationship with Chad. If he didn't love Alyssa enough to give her what she needed, then she didn't need him in her life anymore.

She stretched and then rolled over, spreading herself across the bed diagonally. Closing her eyes, she saw Alex's face in her mind.

Hopefully, he wouldn't be too upset over her being gone in the morning. Chad would let him know that she was safe, and with Zoey still there, he might not even notice her absence.

She would have to ask Rusty how he dealt with the loss. How on earth had he been able to move on? He seemed to be happy enough. In fact, she would have never guessed what he had been through if he hadn't told her.

Memories of Macy filled Alyssa's mind in the dark silence. Tears came. "Why did you go, Macy? Didn't you know how much losing you would kill the rest of us?" She buried her face into the pillow and sobbed. Once the tears stopped—even they had had their limit—she sat up, wrapping her arms around her knees.

It felt good to speak to Macy. If she had died like Alyssa believed, maybe Macy could even hear Alyssa speaking to her. "Macy, I hope you know how much we all love you. Did you know before you took off? Were you only planning on being gone that night? The only thing missing, aside from you, of course, was your favorite purse."

Alyssa sighed. "Was there anything we could have done differently? I would give anything to go back in time and stop you from going. Or let you go and have Zoey and Alex go with you so you wouldn't be alone for a second. Did you mean to leave us? I can't imagine that you did. I know you left that message online, but there's so much doubt around that. Most everyone thinks you were forced to write that. Were you? I hope not. More than anything, I hope not."

She squeezed her knees tighter. "It rips me apart to think about anything bad happening to you. I should have been there to protect you. I tried, I really did. I looked for you until my body hurt. I begged others to help. Your dad, he's been getting the word out on his blog nonstop. And we get along again. We're not fighting anymore, Macy. Well, not until tonight."

Fresh tears filled her eyes, thinking about her fight with Chad. "We can't agree on what to do about you. I don't know if that'll tear us apart or not. I need to give you the memorial service you deserve. What if we never find you? Are we going to never give you a proper service? That's not right. But no matter what happens, Dad and I both love you with all of our hearts. Even if we can't be together anymore." Tears dropped onto her arms.

"Though I think us not being together would hurt Alex more than you. Hopefully, you're in Heaven or someplace good. I can't imagine you going anywhere else. You're so sweet. Feisty, yes." Alyssa couldn't help smiling. "No one could ever doubt your spunk. I'll never forget how mad you got when Dad and I tried to keep you from going vegan. You weren't going to take no for an answer. And you didn't. When I saw you buying your own food, I finally caved. Remember that? I wanted to take you to the gym with me, but you were afraid you'd see kids from school there. You used Dad's weights in the garage."

Alyssa felt a wave of relief wash over her. It felt so good to talk *to* Macy. She really felt like her daughter could hear her. She leaned back and fell into a sleep deeper than she had experienced in a long time.

Stress

MACY LISTENED FOR noise outside the bedroom. Even with her ear pressed against the door, she couldn't hear anything. She would be expected up soon, but she didn't want to see either Chester or Rebekah before she had to.

She held her breath as she opened the door, careful to lift the door up slightly at the just the right spot so it wouldn't squeak. She had managed to open it without a sound yet again. Looking down the empty hall, she pretended she was a ninja as she made her way to the bathroom.

Her leg was fine, though she never did figure out if it had been broken or sprained. It had taken about six weeks to heal, and Rebekah had said she thought that was normal for a broken bone. Macy wasn't so sure, but she was just grateful that she had been walking around for a while.

Although as soon as she could get around, Chester and Rebekah had put her to work. She had to do all kinds of housework and for whatever reason, they still had her studying the community books.

When she was done in the bathroom, she listened to see if they were awake. She'd heard them late into the night. Even though they now lived in a house with every modern convenience, that didn't keep her from hearing their newlywed activities each night.

It disgusted her, but she did her best to keep perspective. It gave her more reason to work on her plan to get out of there. Chester had the house sealed tight. Most of the windows were nailed shut or otherwise made impossible to open. The loud, ear-piercing alarm was set at all times. He hadn't even told Rebekah the code to turn it off.

Looking around, she went into the living room. She walked to the window and peeked around the curtain and moved a blind up. It was light outside and she could see kids her age standing at a bus stop. Most of them were teasing each other and a couple others stood off to the side, looking tired and annoyed.

As much as she had hated school before being kidnapped, Macy would give anything to go back. She would even take the kids who had bullied her. Not only did Chester make them look like scared mice in comparison, but Macy had grown in her confidence. She had survived much more than she ever would have thought possible. She could stand up for herself against some insecure teens.

Macy watched the kids across the street. Had they been Heather's friends?

Heather was part of why Chester had gone so far as to keep their presence hidden from the neighbors. She was locked away at the local mental hospital because of everything Chester had put her through. If Macy was seen, people would know something was up. It was too risky.

Even Chester only went out at night, when he was certain no one would see him. His truck was hidden away in the garage, which had coverings over the windows. Rebekah never left the house either. She was mad about being ripped from the community, and wanted nothing to do with the world.

Macy also knew Rebekah had a warrant out for her arrest from her days in a band. She knew better than to ask Rebekah about it, but she couldn't help wondering if that played into her refusal to leave also.

A noise behind Macy startled her and she jumped back, putting the curtain back in place.

"Do you miss your friends, Heather?" Chester asked. He tied his bathrobe, looking nonplussed.

"Something like that." Pretending to be Heather had become a natural part of life. She no longer wanted to scream that she wasn't Heather.

"Maybe someday you can go outside again and see them," Chester said, referring to the kids outside. "But for now, we have chores. Your true mom is tired from the pregnancy, so you're going to have to do her chores today. Can you handle that?"

Macy held back a groan. "No problem." Doing the extra chores was a small price to pay if it meant keeping Chester's temper at bay.

Macy had expected him to be even angrier with her than he always was already about them being kicked out of the community, but he hadn't been any worse since being in the house. Rebekah was the one who had changed. She had been so kind to Macy before, but now the resentment was all over her face.

"Why don't you start with making breakfast?" Chester asked, his voice cheery. "Then you can take your mom hers in bed."

Macy went to the kitchen. In her real family, breakfast meant either cold cereal or something frozen stuck in the microwave, but living as Chester Woodran's fake daughter, it meant a huge production.

Macy would have to make waffles or pancakes from scratch and then make some kind of complicated egg dish—scrambled, which was easy, was not allowed. The whole thing would make a huge mess, taking her more than an hour to cook and then clean everything. Although she was glad to have electricity again. Living in *the world*, they weren't stuck with the community's insane rules.

The shower sounded as Macy gathered the ingredients. At least she would be left alone for a little bit. Even when Chester wasn't being a jerk, he talked nonstop. He never had anything interesting to say, but he had no shortage of things to rattle on about. Macy knew his thoughts on politics, farming, the news, how people treated him, what life had been like as a child, and a plethora of other topics.

She was sure he loved the sound of his voice so much he had to force others to listen to it also. It might not be so annoying if he wasn't so insistent his opinions were right and anyone who disagreed was wrong.

By the time Chester came into the kitchen again, Macy had everything on the table.

"That smells delicious, Heather. Why don't you grab a tray and take a plate in for your mom?"

Macy's chest tightened. She knew once she got into the bedroom, Rebekah's hate would be felt from across a room.

"Did you hear me?" Chester asked.

"Yes." Macy turned around and went through a couple cabinets until she found the tray he was talking about. She put a plate and silverware on and then filled everything.

She turned around and faced Chester, hoping he would take it into the room instead.

"What are you looking at me for? Take it in to your mom. Be sure to tell her you hope she feels better."

"Okay." Macy did her best to ignore the knots twisting in her stomach. She squeezed the tray and made her way back to Chester and Rebekah's room, dragging her feet. If he said anything about her speed, she would blame it on her leg. He couldn't say anything about that since he was the one who had injured her.

Macy steadied the tray and held her breath, bracing herself. She would go in and out as fast as possible. Maybe Rebekah would even be asleep or at least pretend to be asleep to avoid Macy.

Unfortunately, Rebekah was sitting up with the light on. She was reading what appeared to be a book from the community. Not that she had read anything else that Macy had ever seen.

Rebekah looked up from the large book and shot Macy a disgusted look.

"I've got some breakfast for you." Macy tried to smile, but it didn't quite work.

"Just set it on your dad's side. It won't fit over my belly any more."

Macy nodded, not making eye contact. She walked around to the other side of the bed and pushed the tray closer to her. "I hope you feel better."

"Sure you do."

The words stung. Macy looked at her. "You know, it wasn't my intention to get you kicked out of there. I'm sorry."

"It doesn't matter."

"Yes, it does," Macy said. "We used to get along and—"

"What I meant was that it won't get me back in there. Our entire family has been permanently banned. Jonah, Eve, and the other prophets made that abundantly clear."

"That's not the end of the world. The—"

"Please just go. You're stressing me out."

Macy shook her head and left the room. Why couldn't Rebekah see that the community was a cult? They would probably end up having some mass suicide at some point. She had read in school about that happening to other groups like that.

She went back to the kitchen to find Chester eating. "Is your mom resting?"

"Yes."

"Good. You'd better eat, because we have a lot of chores to do today."

Macy grabbed some food and ate. It should have bugged her that she was comfortable with everything, but it didn't. As much as she wanted to get back to her family, somehow life with Chester and Rebekah had settled into a form of normalcy, even though it sucked. But even when Chester was being nice, it was only so he could catch her off guard when he later snapped.

At first, Macy had been hopeful when he was being nice, but it hadn't taken her long to figure out that it was like the calm before the storm. His politeness made her more nervous than when he was stomping around, complaining.

He set his fork on the plate. The noise startled Macy.

Chester looked into her eyes through his big, ugly glasses. "Today we're going to deep clean. Forget about the laundry and all the other daily chores. Start with the kitchen and then do the bathrooms. By then it should be lunch and we can see how you've done. I'll be in my study."

Macy nodded, biting back a comment. It wasn't fair that she had to do all the work, but she knew better than to say anything. The last thing she needed was to find herself back in the barn or locked back up in Heather's room. Even though she didn't have much freedom, she could at least walk around the house.

She *was* going to get out. Even though Chester kept the alarm on at all times to keep her in, she had a much better chance of getting away here than she had anywhere else. Back at the farm, they were miles away from the nearest people—and that house had been tight with security as well. The community that had proven deadly to escape.

Chester slammed his hands on the table, scaring Macy. "Stop day-dreaming and get to work."

Discovery

MACY FINISHED SCRUBBING the floor in the dining room and then took the supplies back to the laundry room. On her way back, she stopped in the hall, hearing Chester's voice. At first she thought he was talking to her, but then she realized he was on the phone in his study. He wouldn't talk to her in there—he wouldn't let her near the only room with a computer.

She looked up and down the hall, making sure Rebekah wasn't in sight. She pressed her ear against the door, trying to hear what he was saying. It was too muffled to make out more than a couple words in a row. He had to have been trying to speak low, because the way his voice traveled, she could usually hear him from across the house.

He sounded irritated, but that was nothing new. Macy couldn't help being curious. She hadn't heard him talking with anyone since they came to the house months ago. He'd been doing his best to recreate the community by keeping them all secluded from the outside. The only difference was they had electricity.

The only times he left the house were at night to buy *supplies* as he called them. Usually, only groceries, but the way he made such a deal about going out to get them, he had to call them supplies. Like he was a top level spy.

Something slammed in the study and Macy jumped. She ran down the hall on her tip-toes. If Chester was irritated, then she really didn't want him finding her eavesdropping. She went back to the dining room to check the floor for wet spots from mopping. There weren't any that she could see, but she needed to look busy if Chester came by. Her heart still raced and she forced herself to look natural.

A few minutes passed without him returning, and she relaxed. Macy stopped drying the already-dry floor and stood, looking around. There wasn't any noise. She didn't know where he was, but she needed to keep cleaning.

Macy went to the cabinets and dusted, taking down each piece of fine China with care. When she replaced the last one, she turned around and saw Chester watching her. She held her breath, not wanting to show him how startled she was.

He folded his arms and curled one side of his lip. He was giving her such a subtle smirk that it was worse than an outright one. "I have to go somewhere for a little bit."

"In the light?"

"Don't speak unless spoken to. Keep an eye on your mom. She's sleeping now, but she'll probably need something when she wakes. Also, I want you to clean the living room next."

Macy sighed, forcing herself to stay silent. She was exhausted. She'd been deep cleaning for hours and wanted a break. Her body ached, especially where her leg had been injured.

"Is there a problem?"

"No."

"Good. Get to work and don't forget to check on your true mom. And if I'm not home, do you know when to start dinner?"

"Yes."

"Okay. Get to work." He turned around and walked toward the front door. Macy could hear him punching in the code for the alarm. He was making a production of it to get the point across. They both knew the threat of the barn was as real as it always had been.

Macy looked over at the living room in disgust. How could he expect her to keep deep cleaning without a break? He had barely given her any time to scarf down the lunch she made everyone.

Sweat ran down her forehead and she wiped it with the back of her hand, finding it stuck to her hair. She probably looked horrible, not that it mattered. She grabbed the rags from around the room and took them to the laundry, starting another load.

She grabbed some more supplies and went into the hall. Something caught her eye. Macy stared down the hall, trying to figure out what was out of place.

Then she saw it. The door to Chester's study wasn't closed all the way. Was it a trap, or had he let his guard down? She went back to the dining room and looked around for him. He appeared to still be gone. She had heard his car leave the garage, and the fact that he had left while it was still light showed that something was wrong.

Maybe he had left the door open accidentally. Macy looked into their bedroom and saw Rebekah sleeping.

Macy appeared to be in the clear. She took a deep breath, dropping the rags onto the floor. Her heart felt like it was going to pound right out of her chest.

Who knew if she would find anything? But the way he kept it locked up all the time, there was no way she could just leave the room alone. If she walked in and found a camera pointed at her, she could later say that she had been making sure everything was okay since he always leaves the door closed.

She pushed the door open ever so slowly. It creaked slightly, but opened easily enough. Holding her breath, she walked in, not knowing what to expect. She half-expected to see pictures and graphs all over the walls, like she always saw on TV when murderers were stalking someone.

It just looked like a regular home office, though. There was a desk piled with papers. A laptop sat there, screen off. A floor-to-ceiling shelf held books and knick knacks. Papers were scattered on the floor underneath a window with drawn shades.

Macy scanned the room, looking for a hidden camera, but didn't see anything. She knew if there was anything recording her, if she took a step into the room, that would be all it would take for her to end up locked away somewhere. Maybe for good.

She walked over to the desk and looked at the piles of papers without touching anything. The laptop seemed to call her, but she was certain if she got online, he would know. But what if she just looked at some files? Would he know that?

It wasn't a risk Macy was willing to take. She could pick up some papers and he wouldn't know, but he probably had ways he was monitoring his computer.

A crashing noise startled her. Macy jumped and ran to the doorway, looking down the hall. She didn't see anything. Going down to Chester's bedroom, she checked on Rebekah and saw her lunch tray on the floor. She must have rolled over and knocked it down. How had it not woken her?

Macy went over and checked on her breathing and then picked up the mess from the floor. She brought the tray back out to the kitchen and then returned to Chester's study. She looked at the papers sitting on his desk, memorizing their placement. Then she picked up a few, looking through them.

They were all boring. Bills, from what she could tell. She was about to set them back into place when she froze. Now on top of the desk sat a paper with big words on the top: Shady Hills Mental Health Facility.

Was that where Heather had been taken? Was she still there? Heather had never returned to fill out any more of her diaries that Macy could find, so Macy knew nothing beyond the fact that Heather had been sent there.

Macy scanned the paper. The letter was addressed to Chester Woodran, the non-custodial father. So they *had* removed his parental rights. Macy had been right.

He had kidnapped her because he couldn't get his real daughter back.

Macy read it as fast as she could, knowing that she needed to get the living room clean before Chester returned. According to the letter, Heather had behavioral problems and didn't show any signs of being ready to be released.

If Chester had lost his parenting rights, why were they sending him updates? Did he still have some kind of right even though he didn't have custody?

Macy knew time was ticking by. She didn't know where Chester had gone, but she couldn't shake the feeling that she needed to hurry out of the study.

Heather wasn't crazy. She had read the girl's diary entries. Considering she had lived with a monster her entire life and had to deal with the murder of her mom who she'd been so close to, Heather was probably acting out because no one would listen to her. Obviously no one believed Chester to be a murderer if he was being sent updates about Heather.

Maybe together, she and Heather could get him thrown into jail. They definitely could get him for kidnapping. The murder charges would be more difficult if they didn't have a body, but at least they could get him in prison. Surely premeditated kidnapping would be a long sentence.

Macy put the papers back on the desk where they had been. She backed out of the room and looked at the door. It had been left slightly open, but Chester didn't know that. Or did he?

What if he asked if she went in? Her heart sped up. She would have to lie. Not only that, but she would have to practice it until he came back home. She would have to be convincing. Unless he really hadn't noticed.

It was strange that he would be so careless though. It had to be a setup. But she closed the door. Living with him was making her crazy. It was a door. A door. And that was all it took for her to have an argument with herself.

Macy went into the living room and cleaned as fast as she could. Chester wouldn't notice anything because it wasn't a trap. He wouldn't do that because of how protective he was over that room. He wouldn't give her access to it just to see what she would do.

Opportunity

M ACY SAT UP in bed, gasping for air. Sweat dripped into her face, and she wiped it away. She'd had another dream about being locked up in the barn. She squeezed the soft comforter, breathing heavily.

It was just a dream. It wasn't real. Not this time anyway. She hadn't had a dream about going back there in a while. It had to have been the guilt—if that was the right word—about sneaking into Chester's office.

He hadn't said a word about it when he came home. In fact, he'd been distracted about something, not even bothering to criticize the way Macy had cleaned the living room. Usually, he enjoyed pointing out every small thing she hadn't cleaned perfectly.

Her throat was dry and she needed something to drink. The last thing Macy wanted to do was to leave the bedroom and risk running into either Chester or Rebekah. The alarm clock showed that it was just before three in the morning, so the chances of them being up were low, but not impossible.

Rebekah was sometimes up at strange times, especially since she spent most of the days in bed resting. Chester…well, he was Chester. He took pride in being unpredictable, so there was no telling where he would be or when.

Macy's eyes were heavy and it was tempting to go back to sleep, but her throat almost hurt it was so dry. She climbed out of bed, listening for any sound. If she heard anything, she would just deal with the dry throat. There was no way she was going to face either one of them if she didn't have to.

Once she got over the stress of the nightmare, the dryness would most likely go away. But if they were both sleeping, she would rather drink some water and be done with it.

Everything was quiet, so she sneaked into the kitchen and poured water into a cup without making any noise.

After she drank two full glasses of water, she headed back to the bedroom, but before she got there, she noticed a slight breeze before she got to the hall. Why would there be a breeze? Chester didn't open any windows—ever. Most of them were rigged so as to be impossible to open. They had either been bolted or painted shut, plus they were attached to the alarm system.

Macy walked toward the front door. That was where the breeze felt like it was coming from. She looked around and noticed the door to the garage was cracked open.

What was going on? Why was Chester being so careless all of a sudden? Did it have to do with whatever was distracting him? What *was* distracting him?

She pushed the door slightly, half-expecting the alarm to sound even though she knew it wouldn't since it was already open. She peeked in and saw that his truck was gone.

As far as Macy knew, he only left the house about once a week, but now twice in a day?

A noise outside startled her and she jumped. Macy heard the mechanical sounds of the garage door gearing up to open. She closed the door all the way and ran back to the bedroom. Her heart raced and her mouth was dry, despite having just had two glasses of water.

She closed the door and leaned against it, breathing hard, but trying to stay quiet. There was a thud. It sounded like the door to the garage slamming shut.

Macy put her ear to the door. Chester was always talking to himself so maybe he would say something that would tell Macy what was going on. It had to be something big if he was being so careless, leaving the doors open.

His footsteps went down the hall. Macy braced herself, ready to jump into bed and pretend to sleep. He walked past the door, talking to himself as usual. It wasn't anything that gave her any clues. He was only saying something about someone being a complete moron.

That could have referred to just about anyone. He thought everybody was stupid and often expressed his disdain for humanity in general.

Macy thought about his parents. They were so sweet, how could Chester have possibly come from them? His mom was always so nice to everyone. His dad was crotchety, sure, but in an endearing way. He was nothing like Chester.

Her eyes grew heavy again as her heart rate returned to normal. She was too curious to give in. Macy went to the wall that connected to Chester and Rebekah's walk-in closet. If the door was open, maybe she could hear something.

Pressing her ear to the wall, she could hear some muffled shuffling noises, but nothing else. He had to have stopped grumbling to keep from waking Rebekah. Was he trying to keep his middle-of-the-night excursion a secret from her, too?

She froze. Voices. They were speaking to each other. She could only hear two tones, no words. They were both talking, but what were they saying? There had to be a way to find out.

Macy cupped her hands and put them against the wall and listened. It was better, but not by much. She was able to pick up a few words here and there, but not enough to tell her anything. She tried harder, but wasn't able to hear anything.

She had to go to the bathroom. Probably from drinking all that water. That was the excuse she needed. She made her way back to the door and opened it.

Their voices traveled through the hall. If she went a little closer to their door, she might be able to hear what they were discussing. Her heart raced, making it harder to listen. She took several deep breaths as she made her way to their door.

She stood in front of the wall, just next to the door. Rebekah was talking and she sounded irritated. Macy could only make out a few words, but she couldn't make sense of them, so she inched closer.

Now Chester was speaking. "It's better than I thought."

"How can you be sure?" Rebekah asked. "You weren't gone long enough to be able to give a good enough examination. Not only that, but it's dark."

"What would you have me do? Take a day trip?"

"That would make a lot more sense, don't you think?"

"What would I tell Heather? We can't tell her about this yet."

Macy's eyes widened. They couldn't tell her what?

"You don't have to tell her where you're going, Chet. Just tell her you have an errand. You don't owe her an explanation. She's just a child. Tell her you need to take care of something and that I'm in charge. End of story."

"I suppose, but she's going to figure out that something's going on."

"Let her wonder. She'll find out soon enough."

Macy tip-toed closer.

"How are we going to keep her in line? We have to make sure she doesn't try anything."

"You could always lock her up like you've been talking about. But she wouldn't be able to take care of me while you're gone. I can't make my own food. I can barely stand up without getting sick."

"Are you sure I can't take you to a doctor?"

"Doctors are evil, Chet. You know that. The medicines they use, they use them to control people's minds. It's a rough pregnancy, that's all. I've seen it many times back home at the community. What we need is for you to go back to the land and really look at it—in the daylight. Otherwise, we won't really know if it's the right place to start our new community."

The blood drained from Macy's face. They were planning to start a new community?

She walked back to the bedroom and closed the door behind her.

Macy knew deep down in her gut if they entered a new community, she wasn't getting out. Chester would make sure of it, and it sounded as though Rebekah was behind him.

That also explained why she was still studying the community writings. Rebekah and Chester would be the new Jonah and Eve.

If he was going to be gone for an entire day and Rebekah could barely get out of bed, that would be her chance to get away. Chester wouldn't be able to do anything about it.

Macy wouldn't go back to another community. She just couldn't. Escape was her only option, and fast. Macy climbed back into bed, her mind racing but her body exhausted. Her eyes fought to close while every inch of her ached.

How would she get out? Simply go out the front door and let the alarm wail?

Macy pulled the covers up close to her face as the drowsiness took over. She sniffed them, smiling. They smelled so nice and fresh because she had washed all the linens earlier. If nothing else, being kidnapped had taught her to find joy in the little things.

Macy finally gave into her heavy eyelids and thought of ways to escape as she drifted off.

Resolve

C HAD LOOKED OUT the front window again. He expected Alyssa to walk through the door, but it was clear she was serious about going somewhere to get space.

As tempting as it was to call her friends one by one, Chad knew it was a bad idea. She wanted space and if he called, she would push him away even further.

He went upstairs to where Alex and Zoey were doing their studies as usual at the kitchen table.

"Is Mom still sleeping?" Alex asked.

How to answer that one? Chad would have to tell him some version of the truth, but he couldn't bear to give him all of it. Was it because he didn't think Alex could handle it…or because he didn't think he himself could?

Chad cleared his throat. "She's been having a hard time dealing with everything, so she's gone to a friend's house."

"For how long?" Alex asked.

"Until she's able to think clearly."

"Did you two get into a fight, Dad?"

"She just needs space to think. It was too much being here where there are so many memories of Macy. That's all."

Alex didn't look convinced. "If you say so."

"I do. Are you two going to be okay if I go out for a little while? I have to pick up some stuff from the store."

"Whatever." Alex went back his laptop.

Zoey gave Chad a sympathetic look.

"If you guys need anything, I'll keep my cell phone close."

"Okay." Alex didn't look up.

Chad frowned, but didn't say anything. The last thing he needed was for Alex to decide to move into Zoey's house. Not that he would let them stay there alone, but Valerie was due back with Zoey's dad soon and the tables could turn all too easily. Then he would be alone in the house.

He went down to his office and grabbed his cell phone and wallet. Who was he kidding? He didn't know what they needed from the store. Maybe he would get some takeout for lunch and then they could use the leftovers for dinner too. Or he could pick up some milk and eggs.

A lump formed in his throat. He wasn't cut out to do the single dad thing. He also didn't want to do anything to make things worse with the child who was still with him. Hopefully Alyssa would come around because they had been getting along so well before the argument.

He had been excited about the thought of Macy coming back home to find them getting along. He already knew that dream was a long shot, but with Alyssa now thinking that Macy was dead, the dream was nearly crushed.

Even though it did cause a fight between him and Alyssa, he wasn't going to change his stance. He would hold onto his belief until there was hard evidence. And when Macy did get back, she deserved to have a kitchen full of food.

That was it. He would go to the store and buy every vegan item he could find. He would even try some of it. That way, when she got back, they could eat that crazy stuff together, no matter what it tasted it like.

Chad shut off his laptop and went into the garage, on a mission. Maybe he would even grow to like the vegan foods. He knew he could stand to lose a few more pounds. Some weight had come off because he hadn't been eating as much, but there was still room for improvement.

Perhaps if he lost those last few pounds, it would be enough to convince Alyssa to stay home. She was always so fit and healthy, and even though he wasn't what anyone would call overweight, his love handles had to be a turn off for someone as beautiful as her.

He started the car and drove to the grocery store, but before he got there, he saw the natural grocery store that Macy liked so much. He smiled, remembering how she had chattered on about it when they were building it. Yes, that was where he would go.

Pulling into the parking lot, he felt more alive than he had in a long time. Chad was going to win back his wife and have something in common with his daughter when she got back. Since he was on a roll, he knew he would think of something brilliant to bring him closer to Alex also.

He walked through the automatic sliding doors and immediately he felt overwhelmed. This place looked nothing like the grocery stores he went to with Alyssa. To the left, there were enormous displays of fresh fruit, half of which he didn't recognize. To the right was a line of checkout stands. Everyone in line had their own cloth bags, and there wasn't a plastic bag in sight.

His nose tingled. It even smelled different in there. Not bad, just different. He didn't have a clue what the scent was, but he figured it was something natural. He scanned the store, trying to figure out where to begin.

"Hey, stranger."

Chad turned around to see Lydia standing next to him. "You shop here?"

"Of course. My body is a temple." She smiled, flipping her dark hair behind her shoulder. "What are you doing here?"

"Shopping for my family." He put the emphasis on the word family due to their past.

"I would have expected you to go to the discount grocery down the road."

"What's that supposed to mean?"

"Just that you're a pizza and beer kind of guy."

"Yeah, well, I'm trying to change that."

"They sell pizza and beer here too, you know. It's just not what you're used to."

"I'll have to pick some up. Well, I'll see you around."

"This place can be hard to navigate if you're not used to it. I can help you out, and it'll take half the time."

Chad was trying to fix his family. Having his ex-lover show him around the store wasn't the way to go about it. "I can figure it out myself, but thanks."

"If you're sure."

"I am."

"Okay. See you around." She walked away, headed for some kind of star-shaped fruit. He watched as she picked one up and gave it a squeeze and then set it down only to pick up and squeeze another. Lydia put that one in her basket.

She turned around and winked.

Chad turned away and walked toward a shelf full of creams and lotions. He picked one up and pretended that it was the most interesting thing he'd ever seen. Why had he been watching her? It had to have been because he wasn't even sure how to shop in this foreign store.

He put the lotion back on the shelf and went in the opposite direction of Lydia. He wandered the store, staring at brands he had never heard of, although some looked vaguely familiar. Had Macy bought some of those and he'd seen them at home?

Time passed and Chad still hadn't found even one item to place in his basket. How would he ever eat the same items that Macy did if he couldn't even decide what to get? He realized that he wasn't even sure qualified as vegan. He knew she wouldn't eat cheese—how would she eat pizza?—but he wasn't sure what else she didn't eat, aside from meat of course.

The items in front of Chad seemed to be taunting him. Would Macy eat them when she returned? It wasn't even clear, at least to him, what he was looking at. Even though the packaging was in English, it may as well have been Greek.

"You want some help now?"

Lydia. He didn't even need to turn around. "Just trying to decide."

"I can see that. Let me help."

He turned and looked at her for a moment. "Do you really shop here often, Lydia? Or do you follow me? We run into each other an awful lot. I know this isn't the biggest town, but I run into you more than anyone else."

"Great minds." She held up her basket, packed full of fruits, veggies, and an assortment of other things he didn't recognize. "But I really do love this place."

He eyed her basket and then looked at his nearly-empty one. "Oh, all right. But don't read into it, Lydia."

"Me?" She gave him an innocent look and then shook her head. "I'm only here to help a neighbor out."

Right. Chad knew he would have to keep his guard up. Why did he always have to run into her? Was it really just a coincidence? That was likely how they had hooked up in the first place. He couldn't remember for sure, but he wouldn't have gotten together with her if she hadn't kept showing up everywhere.

"So...what is it we're looking for?" she asked.

"Vegan food."

Lydia tilted her head. She had an expression that he couldn't read. She knew about Macy's veganism—Chad had ranted to her about it enough. Did she think he was pathetic since he was out buying food for his daughter who many thought wouldn't return?

She stood up straight. "We're in the wrong section for that. This stuff is full of butter, milk, and eggs. Follow me. I'll show you where they keep what you're looking for."

They went down several aisles and stopped in one that looked almost identical from the one they had started in. "Everything here is vegan. It either has some kind of dairy substitute or is simply made without it. Are you looking for anything in particular?"

He shook his head. "All of Macy's food expired long ago and I want to make sure she has plenty when she returns." If Lydia did feel sorry for him, thinking that he was hanging onto a dream, let her. He didn't need her approval.

"You'll find everything here. Do you want anything else?"

Chad scanned the packages, feeling as lost as before, but at least he knew he was looking at vegan foods. "No. I'm good."

"Glad to help. I'll see you around, Chad." She turned around and took a few steps.

Guilt stung at him for being so rude. "How are you doing, Lydia?"

She turned around and walked back over to him.

"Sorry I didn't ask about you. I was just...distracted. This store is like stepping into a foreign country."

Lydia laughed. "I remember feeling that way."

"How *are* you doing? Does Dean stay home any longer than before?"

"No. You know him. He's really married to his work. I'm not even the mistress."

Was that how Alyssa had felt when he had his job and was getting the blog started?

"Don't worry about me. I'm doing well—keeping busy. How are you holding up?"

Chad frowned. "Just hanging in there. We're waiting on the DNA results."

"Still?" She leaned against a shelf. "I figured the news had moved on and never bothered to update."

"They'll be all over it either way. I don't know if we'll ever get the results, though. It's taking forever."

"Want to talk about it? They have a deli and there are plenty of vegan options, but they also have a ton of meat and cheeses too."

His stomach rumbled loudly and then he looked away.

"Come on. My treat. You look like you have a lot on your mind." Lydia gave him a look that told him she wasn't going to take no for an answer.

Pouring

C HAD BIT INTO his sandwich, unsure what to think of it. He was figured it wouldn't be very filling with only veggies, seeds, and some vegan condiments. He was surprised at the taste. It wasn't bland and gross as he had expected, even though it was still nothing like what he was used to.

He thought of greasy pizza and spicy chicken wings. Would he really be able to give those up? If it would bring Macy back, he would give up anything for life.

"What do you think?" Lydia asked.

"It's good." He picked something out from his teeth. It might have been some kind of sprout, but he couldn't be sure. He wasn't sure that he had ever eaten those before. It looked like grass with a seed at the end. It actually tasted good with the green spread—avocados?

"See? I told you. It's one of my favorites. Sometimes I come here just to have one."

They sat in silence for a few minutes, eating their identical sandwiches. Chad looked around, trying to make sense of the store. Everyone else was bustling around, finding what they needed easily. It reminded him of his first day skiing when everyone else was zooming down the mountain, even preschoolers, and he couldn't get two feet down the bunny slope without biffing it.

"How are things with Alyssa?"

Chad looked at Lydia, startled. She had never asked about Alyssa before, at least not that he could recall.

"You said that you two were working things out. How's that going?"

"It's been going great." He wasn't about to admit the fight to Lydia.

Alyssa would return home, refreshed from a girls' night or two and then they would pick up where they left off.

Lydia raised an eyebrow, probably picking up on the fact that he was leaving out details. They had spent hours upon hours talking. She knew him nearly as well as Alyssa did. "Well, that's good news," Lydia said. "I'm sure Alex is happy about that."

"Yeah, for the most part."

"How's he doing?"

"He's homeschooling right now. With Macy being gone, it was too much for him." Not only that, but also the fact that he was going to be a dad himself soon. What would Lydia think of Chad being a grandpa? He almost laughed. If he wanted to push her away, that might just do it.

"What's so funny?"

Chad looked at her surprised. Had he actually laughed out loud and not noticed?

"You're smiling about something."

"Life just never plays out how we expect, you know?"

"Oh, I know." Chad knew she was referring to the fact that her husband was nothing more than a checkbook and she was the kind of girl who wanted to be treated like a princess—adored and admired. "Anything you want to talk about?"

He shook his head. "Alex has made a bit of a mess of his life, but it'll all work out somehow."

Lydia gave him a knowing look. "He's a teenager now. It's his job to make stupid decisions."

Chad raked his fingers through his hair. "My kids, they take that to the extreme. My parents, when they were alive, used to tell me that one day I would be paid back for the hell I put them through. I didn't put them through anything like this."

Concern washed over her face. "What did Alex do? Kill someone?"

His eyes widened. "Not so loud! Everyone knows who I am, even though they're being nice and pretending not to notice me."

"Sorry. What did he do? I won't tell anyone."

"I really don't want to talk about it."

"You look like you need to."

"No. Really, I don't." He pulled out his phone and checked the time. "I should get back home."

"If you do want to talk, you know my number. We can still be friends. Unless you told Alyssa and…?"

"No!" Chad nearly choked on his sandwich. "Don't ever bring it up to her."

A slow smile spread across her face. "Trust me, that's not something I would ever do."

"I need to get back home. Alex might need some help with his schoolwork or something."

Lydia eyed his basket. "If you need your regular groceries, you should pick up some more food. I can show you—"

"I do need some, but after seeing the prices here, I'll stop off somewhere else to get those."

"Can't say that I blame you." She wrapped up her garbage and stood. "Although if you want your family eating healthier, this is the place to go."

Chad finished off his sparkling water. "If I tried that, I might starve my son. He's particular about his brands."

"I would never guess where he got that." Lydia grinned.

"What's that supposed to mean?"

Lydia laughed. "I saw the way you were eying the stuff here."

"That's because it's like a foreign country." He couldn't help smiling. Talking with her was so natural and fun—and that was a problem, especially with Alyssa already mad at him.

"If that's what you have to tell yourself. I'll see you around. If you ever need anything, don't hesitate to ask, okay? That's what neighbors are for. I mean it."

"Thanks. I'll let you know if I do." He picked up his basket and before he could reach for his trash, Lydia picked it up.

"I'll get that. Take care of yourself."

He nodded and then headed for the registers. He was in dangerous territory and well aware of it. With things as they were, it would be all too easy to pour everything out to Lydia. That had been the problem when they had started talking when he and Alyssa first hit their marital problems.

After checking out, and feeling like an idiot for not having brought his own bag, he decided to go home before stopping off for normal food. He needed to what he bought into the fridge before it went bad, and after eating lunch, the timeframe was growing smaller by the minute.

When he got home, Alex was at the kitchen table by himself. Hopefully he wasn't having trouble in paradise too. "Hey, son. How's it going?"

"Just bombed a quiz, so now I have extra work." He let a dramatic sigh. "I really wanted to be done."

"So take a break. Maybe you'll be able to think clearer when you come back."

"It's so hard to focus. Mom can't even do it. She can barely function, and now she's not even here. Where'd she go? Her phone keeps going straight to voice mail."

Chad's heart sank, but he fought to keep his face straight. "She must be having a good talk with some friends."

Alex scowled. "But she shouldn't turn off her phone. What if we have an emergency? If we need her? You don't even know where she went."

"She's an adult. We can't tell her what to do."

"But she also has a family. She can't forget about us."

"You know Mom. She wouldn't forget about you. This is as hard on us as it is on you. We all have to deal with it in our own ways."

"I know, I know. I'm never going to hear the end of this, am I?"

"Turning your young parents into grandparents? Don't count on that any time soon."

Alex cracked a smile. "Sorry. If it makes you feel any better, I would have made different decisions if I could go back in time."

"If you ever figure out time travel, let me in on it, okay? There are a few things I'd like to do differently myself."

"Like never let Macy go out that night."

"Definitely the first thing I'd take care of. Why don't you relax? Take a nap, maybe. You look like you really need a break."

"A nap? Really?"

"You look like you could use one."

"I'm not three."

"Neither am I, but I really want one." He pulled the first item out of the bag and put it in the fridge.

Alex gave him a funny look. "What's that? It looks like Macy's food."

"I decided to buy some so that when she comes back, she'll have something to eat. We can eat it too. Don't feel like you have to stay away. I bought plenty."

"Why? Are you going to start eating vegan food?"

"I might give it a try. I could stand to lose a few pounds."

"For an old dude, you're in good shape."

Chad looked at Alex for a moment, and he could see his son was worried that he had said something wrong. Normally, Chad would have been offended at being called old, but at that moment, he found it hilarious. A laugh fought to escape.

Alex's eyes widened, watching Chad. He scooted his chair back.

Finally, the laughter made its way out of Chad's throat. Alex jumped. That only made Chad roar all the more. He leaned against the counter, clutching his stomach. It had been so long since he'd laughed—really laughed—that it ached.

He looked over at Alex and saw that he was laughing too. They made eye contact and both went into a deeper fit. Chad's eyes filled with tears and soon ran down his face. He laughed until his gut hurt too much to keep going. He gasped for breath, wiping at his eyes.

When they had both calmed down, Alex gave him a funny look. "It really wasn't that funny."

"I know. We must've needed a good laugh."

"Yeah, I guess so. Sorry I was rude earlier."

"Don't worry about it." Chad wasn't even sure what Alex was referring to. "We're all under stress."

"I think I will take that nap." Alex yawned.

"Where's Zoey? Is everything okay?"

"She just went to her house to get some clothes and stuff."

"You didn't want to go with her?"

He frowned. "Not after failing that stupid quiz. I have to get on track before I fall behind. I have to retake it and pass by tomorrow morning."

"Want me to take it for you?" Chad joked.

"Funny. Not that it would work. They use the webcam to make sure the right person is doing the work."

Chad's sore stomach dropped. "They can't hear us talking, can they?"

Alex shook his head. "I have the mic turned off. They just care about the camera, but I'm surprised they don't want the mic turned on too. I guess they think they could tell if we were cheating."

"Probably. Get yourself that nap. I'm going to take one as well. Maybe by then, Mom will be ready to come back."

The front door opened and Chad looked down the stairs, hoping Alyssa was back already. It was Zoey, with a tear-streaked face.

Reality

THE LOOK ON his dad's face struck terror through Alex's body. He jumped up, expecting to see his mom at the door wrapped in bandages. Instead, Zoey stood there with red, puffy eyes and tear stains down her face. Her hair was messy.

Alex's stomach twisted in knots. "What's wrong?"

"My parents are coming in tonight. They want me to go back home tomorrow. Mom scheduled my next doctor's appointment and she's bringing my sperm donor."

"Your…? You mean your dad."

Anger flashed over her face. "Not my dad. Where's he been? In Japan playing baseball my whole life. He's not a dad. All he's ever done is supply half my genes and some money." She slammed the door. "I told her I'm going to stay here."

Alex's dad sighed behind him. Alex remembered Zoey's mom threatening them with kidnapping charges when Zoey said she would stay at their house instead of going home. His dad was probably worried about that. Probably even more so with his mom out who-knows-where and not even answering her phone.

"Isn't it good that he wants to be involved?" Alex asked.

Zoey shot him a death look and then kicked off her shoes. She stormed up the steps. "It's a little late for that. The stupid jerk never bothered to call me on any birthday or Christmas. Hasn't sent any presents or cards or anything. Apparently, I'm supposed to accept the fact that he sent some money, but you know what? That's a load of crap. Mom's the one who's been here my whole life. He's got another think coming if he wants to walk in and take over the role of a parent."

"Want to do something to get your mind off it?" Alex asked. "I was going to take a nap, but we could watch a movie or something."

"You think watching a movie is going to fix anything?" she demanded.

He backed up. "I didn't say it would fix anything."

"No, I don't want to watch anything. I want to...I don't know. I just...I'm so pissed!"

"What's going to help? You need to calm down. It's not good for the baby."

She narrowed her eyes and stepped closer to Alex. "Don't tell me to calm down. That just pisses me off even more."

"What did I do?" Alex asked.

Her lips formed a straight line and her nostrils flared. "You have to ask?"

Alex sighed. It felt like he was in the middle of one his parents' fights. "Do you want to talk about what happened over there?"

"No. I just want to break something." She stared at him.

"I hope not me."

"Ugh. Let's go watch a movie, but I want to see something in the theater. Something as violent and bloody as possible."

Alex's dad stepped forward. "It's your lucky day, Zoey. There's a gory war movie *and* I happen to be available to drive you guys."

"Sounds good to me." She turned around and put her shoes back on.

Dumbfounded, Alex gave his dad a look of confusion.

Chad shrugged his shoulders and mouthed, "Women."

Alex smiled. Maybe his dad was more relatable than he thought.

Before he knew it, they were across town buying a tub of popcorn as big as his torso, with nearly as much butter and salt. Zoey had gotten a big plate of nachos. Twice she told the guy to put more cheese on it. When they got into their seats, she ate chips with so much cheese on them, he thought they would break.

She caught him watching her. "Want one?"

He shook his head. Her tone told him that he had better not take her up on the offer. "Hopefully, the movie makes you feel better because I don't know how much more of this I can take," he muttered.

"What?" she asked.

"I said I wasn't hungry anyway," Alex said.

Zoey stared at him, as though trying to decide whether or not she believed him.

Luckily for Alex, the room went dark and loud music blared from the speakers on the walls. A screaming army general showed up on the screen and Alex settled into his seat, eating salty, butter-soaked popcorn.

When the movie ended, he looked over at Zoey. The empty nacho tray rested on her lap. Her eyes were closed and she was snoring. So much for not wanting a nap. He turned to his dad. "You wanna wake her?"

He shook his head. "Let's watch the credits. Maybe they have something funny at the end."

"After this movie?"

"You never know."

"Fine by me." He watched the names roll over the screen and realized they would have to agree on a name if they wanted to keep the baby. They had probably discussed it before, but it hadn't felt real until that moment. He looked at the names, hoping for inspiration. But they didn't even know if it was a boy or girl yet, although they would know soon enough.

His breathing felt constricted. What if she did want to keep it? He thought of crying and diapers while trying to do homework. Would they keep with the homeschooling? They would pretty much have to, wouldn't they? He didn't know how much daycare cost, but since neither of them had a job, they couldn't afford it.

Maybe his mom could babysit. She wasn't working either, and it would give her a distraction from thinking about Macy. What grandma didn't love her grandkids? His grandma was always saying that she never saw them enough.

Thinking about his mom as a grandma was weird—almost weirder than thinking of himself as a dad, which was crazy enough.

The credits and music stopped. Zoey sat up, looking around. She rubbed her eyes, knocking the nacho dish onto the floor. "I must have fallen asleep."

Alex bit back a comment about it being a good thing they didn't stay home for a nap. "You wanna go home? To my house, I mean. You can relax in my room or Macy's. Whatever you want to do." He picked up her tray from the floor and dropped in into the canyon that was his popcorn container.

She stretched. "Yeah, maybe we should. I didn't know I was so tired." She struggled to get out of the chair, so Alex held out his hand. Zoey tried again to get out, but finally took his hand. She mumbled a barely-audible thanks and they made their way out into the main lobby.

His dad stopped walking without warning and Alex bumped into him.

"What's going on, Dad?"

He didn't answer. He only stared across the lobby at a group of women.

Alex recognized some of them from the neighborhood. Alex looked over at Zoey. Was it his imagination or did she look irritated? She had been in a better mood after waking. Was she mad at him again? "Dad, let's go. I think we should get Zoey home. Maybe we could stop for ice cream or something." Hopefully that would give him bonus points, and she would stop being upset with him. He wasn't used to it, and he really didn't like it.

Both his dad and Zoey were staring at the women, not answering him. Maybe Zoey wasn't in the mood for ice cream?

One of the ladies broke away from the group and headed their way. She had made them dinner shortly after Macy disappeared. Her name was Laura or something.

She smiled at them as she got closer. "Hi Chad, Alex." She looked at Zoey. "What's your name again, dear?"

Zoey shot her a nasty look. "Zoey."

Alex felt bad for the lady. She hadn't done anything to deserve Zoey's wrath.

Laura smiled anyway. "That's right. Good to see you, Zoey. I'm Lydia."

Oh, Lydia. Alex knew it had started with an L.

His dad was fidgeting next to him. What was up? His dad was one of those people who talked easily with everyone he met. What had his mom always called it? Charisma.

Lydia looked at his dad. "Would you like me to stop by and make some dinner tonight? The HOA hasn't had any sign ups to bring you guys any meals for a long time. You guys seemed to enjoy the lasagna I made last time."

Alex's mouth watered. He remembered that meal. "Yeah. That was delicious. My mom's at a friend's house anyway. We'd probably just eat cereal for dinner tonight."

Both his dad and Zoey shot him a dirty look. What had he done?

Lydia smiled. "That sounds perfect. The girls and me," she indicated toward the other ladies she had been with, "we're going to see that new romantic comedy and then I can come over. You guys just relax and I'll take over the kitchen."

Zoey scowled.

Chad rubbed his hands together, looking nervous. "If you want to. I don't want to put you out."

Lydia twirled a strand of hair. "It's no trouble. Dean's always out of town. It'll be nice to not have dinner alone for a change. Well, it looks like everyone's heading for the movie. I'll see you guys in a few hours!"

The three of them walked to the car in silence. His dad looked deep in thought while Zoey continued to give him the evil eye.

What was so wrong with having her make their dinner? His mom obviously wasn't going to make anything, and Lydia would have been home alone, anyway. She may as well make them her lasagna. His stomach rumbled just thinking about it.

When they got home, his dad announced he was going to check his blog comments. He went downstairs and Alex followed Zoey upstairs. When they got to the bonus room, she stared at him. "How could you do that?"

"Do what?"

"Encourage her to make dinner over here."

"So we can have a delicious home-cooked meal. I don't remember if you ate her lasagna or not, but it was one of the best things I've ever eaten. And I'm not just saying that. Would you rather have frozen waffles?"

"Actually, yes." She sat down on the couch and turned on music videos.

Alex sat next to her. "Why?"

Zoey narrowed her eyes. "Are you really that blind?"

"Apparently I am. Want to fill me in?"

Zoey stared at him. "Have you noticed the way she looks at your dad?"

"What? She's married. He's married."

"Like people don't have affairs."

"Not my parents."

"She thinks your dad is hot and neither of their spouses are home tonight."

"Get your mind out of the gutter. There's no way she wants to be with my dad. That's just gross."

"I know you see him as just your dad, but one thing you need to realize is that he's hot."

"You think my dad's hot?" Alex's voice squeaked.

She rolled her eyes. "Look, he's practically like my own dad. He's more of a dad to me than that jerk of a sperm donor. I'm just stating the facts. For a guy his age, he's sexy. When Lydia's here, watch how she looks at him. She wants him like you want that lasagna."

Alex shook his head. "No, that's not possible. It's also disgusting. Besides, even if she does think he's hot, she knows they're both married. There's no way."

"You're so naive."

"Am not."

"Are too. She's looking for love. Her husband must never be home, because every time I've ever seen her, he's out of town. Your dad's an easy target. He's dealing with a missing daughter and if your mom is out of the house tonight...."

"Fine, let's not leave them alone tonight. Okay? We'll suffocate them until she goes back home, and then you'll see."

"Actually, you'll see," Zoey said.

Nerve

MACY SAT AT the kitchen table pretending to do her *community* studies. At least Chester was giving her a break from all the cleaning. It gave her a chance to think about her escape plan, which was essentially nothing at this point. She had fallen asleep as soon as she closed her eyes the night before.

"What's this?"

She looked up to see Chester standing where the dining room and hall met. He held up her—Heather's—bedding.

Macy tried to keep sarcasm out of her voice. "A bed spread."

"A bed spread?" Chester shouted.

Her heart sank. He was in a rage again.

Chester walked up to her, holding the covers close to her. "Just a bed spread?" His face was red and he had that scary look in his eyes again.

Macy nodded, her stomach twisting in knots. Was he going to lock her up because of some issue with the bedding, so they wouldn't worry about her trying to escape while he was gone?

"That's all you have? Really?"

"What do you want me to say?" Macy blinked back tears. She didn't want to be locked up somewhere. Had she been stupid to get her hopes up about getting away? She should have known he would have a plan other than keeping her in with Rebekah and an alarm system.

"Do you call this clean?"

"What?"

"Your covers, Heather. They're atrocious," Chester growled. He held them up to his face and gave her a disgusted look. "You were supposed to wash all the linens yesterday."

"I did."

"Did you? It doesn't smell like it to me. Does it to you?" He shoved them into her face. "Smell!"

Macy didn't have to. The stench hit her before the covers touched her face. They reeked of body odor. It smelled like an entire football team had rolled around on them after playing a game.

"Is that clean?"

She shook her head no. How had they gotten so gross? Macy had washed them. In fact, she remembered how fresh they had smelled the night before. Before going to sleep, she had even enjoyed the fresh, clean smell.

"That's right! They don't smell clean. Do you need a lesson in laundry?" he shouted. His spit landed on her face, but she knew better than to wipe it away. "How could you think these were clean? Tell me!"

"They were clean," Macy whispered.

"What did you say?"

"They *were* clean."

"You call this clean?"

She shook her head. "They didn't smell like that before."

"What are you trying to say?" He grabbed her shirt and pulled her out of the chair.

Macy looked away. "I don't know what happened, but when I washed them, they were clean. I smelled them last night, and they were fresh."

"Are you telling me that I don't know what I'm talking about?"

"No."

"Don't lie to me. Tell me you screwed up."

"But I didn't. When they—"

"I *said* tell me the truth." He shoved her into the table, jamming her side into the corner.

Macy gasped in pain. "I am. It was clean. I smelled it myself."

Chester shoved her farther into the side of the table. "Then how did it get like this?"

"I don't know."

"Are you not bathing properly? Did you make them smell like this?"

"No. No." She shook her head while tears blurred her vision.

"What is it then? Do you need lessons on showering or laundry? Which is it?"

Macy looked away, not answering. She didn't need instruction on any of that.

"Don't ignore me." He squeezed her shirt tighter, causing the collar to choke her. "What do you need a lesson on?"

He let go of her shirt, causing her to fall. She hit her shoulder and head against the table as she slid down to the floor, gasping for air.

"What do I need to give you lessons on?"

"Laundry."

"So you admit that you didn't wash the linens correctly?"

Looking away, she nodded.

"I can't hear you!"

"Yes," she said as loud as she could muster.

Chester grabbed her arm and yanked her up. "Why couldn't you have just admitted that in the first place?" He shoved the covers against her face. "Make sure they don't smell like that again. Do you understand?"

"Yes."

He dragged her to the laundry room and her feet stumbled, trying to keep up. He threw the bedding into the front loader and slammed it shut. "The first thing you have to do is make sure what you're washing is in the washing machine. Is that too complicated?"

"No."

"Good. Don't mess it up again." He picked up the bottle of laundry detergent and read the instructions verbatim. "Shall I show you?"

Macy nodded.

He pulled off the lid with dramatic flair and brought the bottle inches from her. "Watch as I measure." He poured the liquid to the second line and then poured it to the machine. "This is the correct setting for linens." He spun the dial around. "Next we make sure everything else is on the proper setting." He pushed the rest of the buttons, explaining the importance of each one as he went along.

"Do you think you can replicate that in the future?"

"Yes."

"Or would you rather I write down instructions?"

"No."

"Good. Now, get back to your studies. It's important you understand everything contained within the books."

"Okay." She turned around and went back into the dining room, blinking back tears. She had cleaned all of the bedding the right way. There was no way she would have been able to sleep in her bed if they had smelled that foul the night before. Whatever had happened to them, it wasn't her fault. Not that it mattered, because she was the one who was getting in trouble for it.

Chester walked by her without a word and got a drink of water from the kitchen. After he put the glass in the dishwasher, he walked to the table and stared at Macy. "I'm going to take a shower. When I get out, we're going to have a little quiz about your reading. Understand?"

Macy nodded, afraid to speak. She knew if she said a word, she would dissolve into tears.

"Good." He walked away, and as he did, Macy got a whiff of body odor.

Anger burned within her. He had to have rubbed her clean covers all over himself, making them stink. Then he turned around and yelled at her, making her feel like she had done something wrong. All along, he had known that it wasn't her fault.

He had to have been trying to break her down to make sure she wouldn't go anywhere while he was away.

Unfortunately for him, his plan had backfired. Macy now wanted to get back home even more than before. Determination ran through her. She would find a way of escape before Chester dragged her back to another community.

The sounds of the shower starting startled Macy. Was this her opportunity? Sure, he wasn't miles away, but he was in the shower. Macy would have the advantage. She was fully clothed and he wasn't. Surely he wouldn't run after in the nude. Or would he?

She got up and looked down the hall. The door was closed and she could hear him banging things around in the shower. Her heart pounded nearly out of her chest. This was it. It had to be. She was *done* dealing with his abuse.

Barely able to walk straight, she went to the line of shoes by the door and put hers on. They weren't the best running shoes, but they were better than nothing.

Macy looked down the hall again, this time shaking violently. She could barely see straight and her fingers and feet felt cold.

The shower was still going, but probably not for much longer. If she waited too long, she'd lose her chance. She took a deep breath and placed her hand on the knob of the front door. It was now or never.

She swallowed, her dry throat not allowing any movement. Her hand clung to the knob as she turned it. Macy pulled the door toward her. The alarm screamed and wailed, notifying everyone within a several block range of what she had done.

Her feet moved into motion before she had time to think. She pushed the screen door open and she was out in the sun. The air was chilly, but the sun itself felt good. When had the last time been when she was able to go outside?

Macy made her way across the yard and went left down the street. The alarm still screamed, and Chester was bound to be after her in a matter of moments. All he would have to do was get out of the shower and throw on some pants.

There was no way he could be surprised that she would escape after how he had just treated her. It was almost as though he was testing her.

She kept looking back, expecting to see him. It was only a matter of time. She turned down another street.

"Heather!" called someone from a yard.

Macy turned and saw a girl about her age waving.

"Stop, Heather! What are you doing home? When did you…?"

The voice trailed away as Macy picked up her pace. With that fool yelling Heather's name, Chester would know what direction she went. She looked for another street to go down, but came to a dead end.

She couldn't turn around. She would either have to hide or go through someone's yard to get to the street behind. She could still hear the sound of the house alarm wailing. If Chester had that hooked up, the police would be coming soon. That could be good or bad.

If they found her first, she could tell them that Chester had kidnapped her. Then maybe they would take her home. Although if they went to the house and talked with him or Rebekah first, they would probably say she had tried to run away. What if they forced her to go back? What if they wouldn't listen to her like they hadn't listened to Heather?

She ran through the yard in front of her and went around to the side of the house. There was a gate, but no latch. She reached around, scratching her arm on the fence. She found the latch and unhooked it.

A dog barked and ran past her for the street. There was no time to feel bad about the dog escaping. She ran into the yard and looked for a way over the fence. She saw a plastic climbing toy. It was just high enough, so she pushed it up to the fence and climbed on top. Then she grabbed the top of the fence and climbed up. She looked into another back yard.

Voices could be heard not far away from the street behind her. She should have closed the gate; everyone would know she ran into that yard. She braced herself for the jump, knowing that her leg was still weak. If she landed wrong she could reinjure it, but there was no time to worry.

She jumped, preparing to land on her good leg and then roll. Macy landed on a patch of grass and somehow managed to avoid hitting her bad leg. She rolled a few times and then jumped up and ran for the next gate. Her knee stung a little, most likely because she hadn't been outside to run or even walk much. The only 'exercise' she had gotten in a long time was housework.

Ignoring the pain, she got the gate open and made sure to close it. She wasn't going to leave a blatant path for Chester to follow.

Sirens blared in the distance over the sound of Chester's house alarm. Macy needed to get to them before Chester did. Otherwise, he would tell them that she was Heather and had run away. She could explain that she'd been kidnapped, but the police might not believe her. Chester had pictures that looked just like her all over his house.

Macy ran to the edge of the house. She hid and also looked up and down the street. At least this road wasn't a dead end. She could go down the opposite way and get away from Chester and the sirens and alarm.

There wasn't anyone out on the street. Macy took a deep breath and made a run for it. She went down the street as fast as she could, keeping an eye out for another place to turn so that she could hopefully get out of the neighborhood. Once out, she would decide her next step.

The road curved up ahead, going toward Chester's house. Macy wanted to go the other way, but that meant going through more yards and she would rather take her chances with the open road. It might curve again or even cross another one, giving her a way out.

Perhaps going back to Chester's house wasn't such a bad idea. If the police weren't talking to him yet, she could tell them that he was a madman who had kidnapped her from her family.

Macy took a couple steps, but then heard yelling from behind her, and the sirens were getting louder and closer. They were going to be headed for Chester's house. He would undoubtedly tell them she was Heather and she was running away. He would probably even have some crazy story, making her sound dangerous.

She gasped for air. Why wasn't there a cross street? The road was probably going to loop around and leave her face to face with Chester.

"There you are!"

Macy looked over to see Chester heading her way.

Determined

MACY'S HEART STOPPED for a moment. Chester was about a block away. She turned around and ran faster. Her sore leg protested, but she didn't care. She would take care of it later.

He was yelling something at her. Macy turned her head back and saw that he was only wearing pants. She had been right in guessing he would throw some on and go after her.

"Stop, Heather! We need to talk about this."

Macy pushed herself to go faster. Her lungs and calves burned while her knee protested. It didn't matter. He would kill her if he brought her back to the house. Any injuries she incurred running would heal.

"Heather, wait!"

She looked back. He was getting closer. "No!"

Macy forced herself to run even faster. She passed the house that she had used to go through the back yard. Macy pushed forward. She would get away. There was no other option.

Fingers brushed against her back.

Macy screamed both from terror and in hopes to startle him enough to back off. She ran ahead, forcing her body to go faster. Letting him catch her was not an option. No matter what it took, he was not going to lock her up again. Chester was done controlling her and scaring her into submission.

He could do what he wanted to Rebekah. She had moved into the house willingly. She saw the way Chester treated Macy. She had been in a rock band at one point. Somewhere within her was the ability to see what was really going on.

She felt a tugging sensation on her shirt. Chester had her shirt. Macy threw herself to the ground, forcing him to let go. She tumbled and then rolled over the hard pavement and a couple rocks that were definitely going to leave bruises.

Chester yelled out at her. She looked over at him as she stopped rolling. He was falling toward the ground—it looked like it was happening in slow motion—and he was headed for her. The last thing she needed was him crushing her.

Macy rolled one more time. As she did, he slid across the pavement. First his arm hit and then he rolled onto his chest, still sliding forward. Then his cheek hit the ground, sending his big, ugly glasses flying. He rolled onto his back, exposing his now-bloody bare torso.

He moaned and then sat up, patting the ground. "Where are my glasses?"

Macy jumped up and ran, but then she stopped. "You need your glasses, Chester?" She didn't wait for an answer. Macy went over to where they rested, picked them up, and then chucked them into the yard. "Go and find them. I could have crushed them, but you know what? I'm going to be nice, unlike you. If you were a nicer person, you wouldn't have to force people to act like they love you. Heather used to love you. Her mom, too."

Macy turned around and ran, unsuccessfully trying to ignore her knee. The pain was worse. At least Chester was behind her and would take a while to find his glasses.

The sirens grew louder, but they didn't sound like they were moving any more. The cops had to have already arrived at Chester's house. The road curved and she found herself looking at several cop cars parked in front of the Woodran residence.

Did all roads lead to that house? Panic rushed through her. If she turned around, she would have to face Chester. She saw Rebekah standing on the front porch talking to a couple officers.

Macy's only way out was to go past the house and the cops. If Rebekah saw her, it would be over. As far as she knew, Macy was Heather.

"Heather!" shouted someone from behind.

Without thinking, Macy turned around. A lady about her parents' age stood behind her. She was wearing what looked like nurses' scrubs. They had cartoon puppies on them.

An officer came out of one of the cruisers. He looked back and forth between the nurse and Macy.

"Is this the runaway?"

The nurse looked confused. "Runaway? This is Heather Woodran. She's a patient over at Shady Hills where I'm a nurse. I'm Candice Roberts."

Macy's heart sank. She looked for a way to escape.

"I was told that she ran away from home," said the officer. "That's what set off the alarm."

Candice shook her head. "She had to have escaped Shady Hills. There's no way she was released. Heather has been…well, having issues. That's all I can say legally. Also, her dad lost custody and can only see her with supervision. I have no idea how she got here, officer, but I assure you she needs to get back to Shady Hills. You're going to want to look into how he got her out."

"But I'm—" Macy said.

"Heather, stay quiet if you know what's good for you," said Candice.

"I'm not—"

"How do you feel about going back into solitary? It won't just be for a couple days this time."

Macy's eyes widened. What had Heather been through? Macy would have to stay quiet for the time being. There would have to be a better time to explain who she really was.

The officer scribbled notes onto a tablet with a stylus. "If that's the case, I'll have to drive her back."

"I'm on my way to work now. I can take her. It's no problem." Candice wrapped a hand around Macy's arm and squeezed.

Why was freedom so fleeting? There was no way she could break away and outrun a nurse and a cop.

"Let me call down to Shady Hills and if what you say is true, I'll release her into your care." He pulled a smartphone out of his pocket. "You two stay right there." He walked over to his car, talking on the phone.

Candice squeezed Macy's arm tighter. "How did you get out? That place is sealed up tight."

Macy glared at her. "Maybe it's not as secure as you thought. Or maybe you underestimated me."

"You're going back into solitary for this."

Macy shook her head. "Trust me, after everything I've been through, you can't scare me."

"How dare—?"

The officer walked back to them. "The office at Shady Hills confirmed that Heather Woodran is a long-term patient and you're one of her overseeing nurses, Mrs. Roberts. I'll just need to see your identification, and then if you sign here, you're free to take her."

Candice gave Macy a dirty look. "Gladly." She pulled out her driver's license and then took the tablet and signed with the stylus, all without letting go of Macy. When she handed the tablet back to the officer, she yanked Macy's arm and pulled her across the street.

Chester came down the street with a limp of his own to go with his bloody torso. His glasses were also crooked. "Hey, Candice! What are you doing with Heather?"

"Taking her back to Shady Hills—where she belongs. Go get yourself cleaned up, Chet. What the hell happened to you, anyway?"

"None of your business. Hand her over. I'll take her."

Macy stood closer to Candice. No matter how mean she seemed, Macy would rather go with her than Chester.

"We all know you lost custody," Candice said. "I'm not going to jail over you. Pull your life together and get custody back, then you can have her."

Chester furrowed his eyebrows. "Hand her over now."

The look in his eyes shot terror throughout Macy. "He's not even my dad! He kidnapped me. Get him away!"

"Kidnapped you?" Candice gave her a bewildered look. "Have you forgotten that I've known you your whole life? Your mom was pregnant with you when we met. I brought your parents dinner the night they came home from the hospital. You really need to get your crap together, kid, or you're never going to leave Shady Hills."

Chester reached out for Macy.

"Officers!" Candice shouted.

"I'm going home." Chester narrowed his eyes. "Don't think you've heard last of me. Any of you."

Candice gave a bitter laugh. "I would never think that, Chet. Go get yourself cleaned up and take care of that pregnant girl on your steps. No wonder you've all been hiding away in there." She shook her head and dragged Macy into a little silver sports car. "Buckle up and don't try anything. There are three police cars right there. I won't hesitate to have them take you downtown, and trust me, you don't want to go there. It makes Shady Hills look like the Hilton."

Macy pulled her arm away from Candice's grip. She got in without a word. At least she was getting away from Chester, and hopefully for good. What would happen when they got there and realized there were two Heather Woodrans?

As they drove to the mental hospital, Macy looked all around for clues as to where they were. It was hard to focus because Candice kept lecturing her about her behavior.

Finally, Macy turned and looked at her while they were at a stop light. "What exactly do I have to look forward to? My mom is dead, not that anyone will listen to me about that. My dad doesn't have custody, not that I'd really want to stay with him anyway."

"You would either stay with extended family or go into foster care. There are a lot of really nice families. You'd even be able to go back to school, although at this point, you would be really far behind."

"Why won't anyone listen to me about my mom?"

"Because we know she's alive."

That was impossible. "How do you know that?"

"We've talked with her." Candice shook her head, looking irritated.

Everything seemed to shrink around Macy. "You did? When? Why haven't I talked to her?" Or had Heather actually talked with her? If so, what was she still doing in Shady Hills?

"Have you actually forgotten? You did, but you tried to convince us that it wasn't her."

"And you didn't believe me? I'm her daughter. I'd know a fake Karla Woodran more than anyone."

"I spoke with her too, Heather. Don't forget how long I've known her."

Macy folded her arms. It was pointless to keep arguing with the woman. Chester had obviously found someone who sounded just like Heather's mom to talk with people over the phone. That explained how he was able to avoid jail. Poor Heather. Talking to someone who sounded like her mom had probably crushed her, and then having no one believe her that it wasn't her mom probably sent her over the edge. No wonder she was still there.

Heather was probably having a worse time than Macy. They'd both been ripped from their families, but she knew her mom was dead. Macy at least knew there was hope of seeing her family again.

"Did I finally render Heather Woodran speechless?" Candice asked, her tone full of snark.

Macy glared at her, but didn't say anything. Whatever she did say would just dig herself—and Heather—deeper. What she needed was to find a way to get the both of them out of the hospital. It wasn't going to be an easy task, but at least they would be able to put their heads together when Macy got to Shady Hills.

Candice pulled the car into a parking lot. The building was several stories tall and though it was clean and well-kept, it gave Macy the chills. They got out and Macy thought about taking another run for it, but she had a limp and her body ached from earlier. Besides, she needed to talk with Heather, and going in was her only way of doing that. They would find a way out together.

She followed Candice, keeping her gaze toward the ground. She had become accustomed to that from living in the community, since she wasn't supposed to look at any guys without their permission. But it worked here too, because she didn't want anyone figuring out that there were two Heathers.

They walked by a large registration desk. Clearly no one had any questions about Candice being with Heather. Then Candice pulled out a card and scanned it in front of a large, metal door. It opened slowly and they went inside, the door closing on its own behind them. They went through several more doors just like that one.

Macy started to doubt their escape. Unless Macy or Heather could sneak one of the cards from someone. There were two of them. One could stay in the room while the other sneaked out to get a card. Maybe they did have a chance.

Candice and Macy came to another desk, but this one was smaller and didn't have anyone sitting at it. Candice grabbed Macy's arm and led her down a hall. They went into a room marked 108.

Candice glared at her. "You stay in your room. Do you understand? I can lock it from the outside, and probably should. I don't know how you got out, but you're lucky that I'm the one who found you. I don't want you sent to the third floor. We'll just pretend this never happened. I don't think the police officer actually made any kind of report when he called in about you. He just asked if you were a resident and if I was a nurse. Next time, I won't be so lenient. Are we at an understanding?" Her eyes narrowed.

"Yeah."

"Not even a thanks? Why am I surprised? Look, Heather. Just get your street clothes off and stay in here. Do us both a favor."

Worried

ZOEY FROWNED, SITTING on Alex's bed. The dinner had gone seamlessly, and Lydia had been on her best behavior, not giving any indication that she had any feelings for Chad.

"See?" Alex asked. "There was nothing to worry about."

"Don't look at me like that," Zoey said. "Lydia only acted like that because we were so close. This won't be the last of her."

"If she does show up again, then I'll keep watch, okay? But she just acted like any other neighbor who came over with dinner when Macy disappeared. Remember? You were there."

"Yeah, but she's the only one who stayed to eat with us, right?"

"She's lonely. You heard her talk about her husband. She said he's home three nights a month if she's lucky. Remember?"

"Right. She's lonely and your dad's hot."

"Stop calling my dad hot. And Lydia's not available. She's married."

"You're not usually so naive. What gives?"

"Quit calling me that. Shouldn't we work on our homework?" Alex asked. He looked eager for a new topic of conversation.

Zoey could feel tears threatening. "Why can't you leave me alone? My life has been crumbling around me for months now, getting worse with each passing month."

"You think mine isn't?"

"Not like mine is!"

"How so? My *sister* has been gone without a trace. I'm thirteen and going to be a dad. Now my mom won't come home."

Rage ran through Zoey. "Your missing sister is my best friend! Yeah, you're going to be a dad, but you're not the one getting bigger every day.

I'm going to have to buy new shoes. You know why? Because even my feet are fat. People don't look at you and automatically know you're going to be a parent. I'm a neon sign for teenage pregnancy."

"Yeah, but when you wear flowing shirts like that one, it's not that noticeable."

"You don't know anything!" She got up and stormed out of the room. He followed her. "What do you mean?"

"It means you didn't notice anyone pointing at me when we were at the movies today. You didn't hear what people said, loud enough for me to hear." She blinked back tears. What she wouldn't have given for a cigarette.

"Nobody said anything. If anyone had, I would have gotten in their faces and if necessary, beaten the crap out of them."

"Well, you know what? They did, and you weren't my knight in shining armor."

"What did they say?"

"Forget it, Alex. It's pointless. People were calling me a whore right under your nose and you didn't even notice."

"Why didn't you say anything?"

"Because the only thing I wanted was to get away from them. They were on their way out as we were going in. Besides, we can't fight everyone. Are we going to fight every time we go into public?"

"If people are going to call you names, then yes."

"That's why we left school. The best thing is probably for me to stay away from places like the movies and the mall. It's only a matter of time until the news picks up on this. I'm surprised they haven't yet."

"It's because they don't care about Macy anymore."

"My point is that I don't want to go out. At least the news isn't hounding you guys. That's, like, the one good thing going on."

"What about me?" Alex looked hurt.

"You? What about you?"

"Aren't I a good thing?"

Zoey frowned. "Most of the time."

"So, I'm not now? Is that what you're saying?"

"If the shoe fits."

He opened his mouth and then shut it.

"If you have something to say, say it."

"Zoey, I don't want to fight."

"Say it!"

Alex looked frustrated. "I'm not trying to compare who's having a harder time, okay? I know you love Macy like a sister. I know the pregnancy is obviously harder on you. Probably in a lot more ways than I think. You're the one solid in my life with everything else falling apart. I really don't want to fight."

"It's a little late for that." Zoey stormed to Macy's room.

"Are you going to stay there tonight?" Alex asked.

"Yep." She slammed the door behind her. She locked it and threw herself onto the bed, finally allowing the tears to fall. It felt like the world was crushing her, and arguing with Alex only made things worse. How could he have not seen those jerks pointing at her and calling her names?

She sat up and looked around Macy's room which had almost become hers.

Scratching noises brought her attention to the ferret cage. The cute, little face stared up at her. Ducky begged for attention. Sighing, she opened the cage and he ran down the levels and into her lap. He jumped around, making Zoey laugh, despite everything else. She picked him up and carried him to the bed.

Ducky scampered across the bed, hopping around like a flea. The poor thing was attention-starved. She hadn't paid him much attention, and she doubted anyone else had, either, aside from cleaning the cage. He darted under the covers and she watched as he moved around, making the blankets go up and down in the process.

She peeked into his cage—the litter box had piled up and the food dish was empty. Zoey wasn't supposed to clean any litter boxes—doctor's orders—so she would have to tell Alex or Chad. But she had to feed the poor thing.

Keeping her attention on the bouncing covers to make sure he didn't escape, Zoey got up and grabbed the bag of food and filled the food dish.

When she sat back down, Ducky popped out of the covers. He climbed up her shirt onto her shoulder and went around the back of her neck to the other side, tickling her. He got caught in her hair, so she had to pull him out, untangling her hair in the process.

It was nice to have the distraction. Ducky was so cute, and the way he jumped around was hilarious. If her life didn't suck so much, she would have laughed at him. Once free of her hair, he jumped around on top of the covers for a while, a few times trying to run down the bed, but Zoey grabbed him each time. The last thing she wanted to do was to have to chase him around the room.

When Macy had first gotten him, he had gotten stuck—or just enjoyed hiding—inside of the dresser behind a drawer. The two of them had spent hours chasing after him, trying to get him out. He darted through the drawers, out onto the floor, around the room, and back into the dresser again.

That was why Zoey was so careful not to let him off the bed. It had been hard enough for two of them to catch him, she didn't want to do have to chase him through the room on her own. He seemed to have more energy than ever before, and that was saying a lot for a ferret. He slept most of the day, cram-packing all that energy into a few short hours.

She was about ready to put him back in the cage when he dawdled over to her and snuggled against her bulging belly. Zoey leaned back and stroked his little body while he snuggled against her.

"You miss her, too? How are we going to get her back?" Zoey sat there, petting him until he fell asleep. "What are we going to do about anything?" Zoey's eyes got heavy and she didn't want to fall asleep and have Ducky wake up and get lost, so she put him back in the smelly cage and then climbed into Macy's bed, too tired to care about the stink of the litter box.

When she woke up, it was dark and she had to go to the bathroom really bad. She remembered when that intruder had broken into the Mercer's house, knocking Zoey out and leaving her in their garage. She held her breath, not wanting to go out.

The doctor had warned her flashbacks could occur at any time, even if it had been a long time. It had been months and she had almost forgotten about it, but she was terrified to go into the hall. She had been going to the bathroom in the middle of the night for a while with no problems.

She also knew the Mercer's had bought a top of the line security system and still had the police keeping an eye on the place. Even though they didn't park out front anymore, they made a point to drive by often enough, especially at night.

The pressure on her bladder urged her to get out of bed. She slid her swelling feet onto the floor and tip-toed to the door. She put her ear against it, listening. The only thing she could hear was the sound of her own labored breathing.

Zoey opened the door, half-expecting to see the man standing there with a knife. Yes, she had an active imagination, but there was good reason for it this time. The hall was empty and dark, only lit with a night light several feet away. It was enough to see she had nothing to worry about.

She went to the bathroom and then considered going to Alex's room. She was still ticked at him for being so dense. Even if he hadn't heard what those kids had said at the theater, he should have believed her. He had been acting like such a buffoon, but she still wanted to be with him.

Tip-toeing again, she went to his room and slid the door open. The room was dark and she could hear his heavy breathing, so she closed the door behind her—not that Chad would care that they were in there together. Alyssa would, but she wasn't there.

Sliding in next to him, she made herself comfortable under the covers. She remembered the Star Wars sheets he'd had to put on the bed when the laundry had piled up. Alex had been really embarrassed, but Zoey was more impressed that they had found them in the queen size.

Alex stirred next to her. "Zoey?"

"Yeah." She moved closer to him, feeling her anger melt away.

He wrapped an arm around her. "You're not mad at me?"

She shook her head, not actually answering.

"I love you," he whispered and then his breathing slipped back to what it had been. She listened to the rhythm for a few minutes before falling asleep herself.

Mirror

MACY STOOD AT the window of Heather's room in the hospital. It was late, but she couldn't sleep. Heather still hadn't come back to the room, although she did see another nurse, who came in looking surprised.

She had said, "Heather, what are you doing here? I thought you were still on the second floor."

Macy smiled. "Got off on good behavior."

The nurse's eyes widened. "Really? Well, that's certainly good news." Then she had brought Macy dinner, which wasn't very good, but was at least something in her stomach. And it was something that Macy hadn't had to cook herself.

That had been hours ago. Candice had checked on her a couple times, but said she was busy with other patients. Macy was anxious to meet Heather, the girl she had been pretending to be for months. The girl who no one questioned was her, not even her grandparents or her neighbor who had known her since she was a baby. Even Macy, when looking at Heather's pictures, had a hard time believing they weren't of her. She had seen twins who had looked less alike than Heather and her.

The door opened and Macy jumped. She ran to a corner and slid down to the floor. Someone was shoved into the room. "Stay there and be good. You don't want to go back to the second floor, Heather. I'm locking the door, but hopefully tomorrow we won't have to." The door slammed shut and Macy heard the lock go into place.

Her heart picked up speed. How was she going to introduce herself to Heather?

Heather swore and then turned on the light. She turned around and froze when she saw Macy. "Who the...? What? Is this some kind of trick? Are they trying to—?"

Macy stood up. "Heather, I—"

"Are they trying to mess with me? Who are you and why do you look exactly like me? Even your hair!" She picked up a book and held it as though it were a weapon. She stared at Macy. "You look *just* like me. What's going on?"

"Let me explain. Please."

Heather lowered the book slightly, giving Macy a suspicious look. "I guess I have nothing better to do. But first, who *are* you?"

Macy held her hands up slightly, showing her that she wasn't going to hurt her. She sat in a chair. "It's a long story. You might want to sit."

"This should be good." Heather sat on the bed, not taking her eyes off Macy.

"My name is Macy Mercer and your dad kidnapped me to replace you."

Heather's face appeared to soften. "What?"

Macy wrung her hands together. "He found me online and pretended to be someone else—a teenage boy—so I would meet him. When I did, he kidnapped me. He locked me up until I agreed to call him Dad." Macy went on to explain some of what Chester had put her through, describing him and her grandparents so Heather would know she wasn't lying. She even described the farm house and the house she had just left.

The book dropped from Heather's hands and hit the floor. "He replaced me?" Her eyes shone with tears. "What about Mom? Did he replace her, too?"

"Yeah, he replaced her too, with a younger model. I'm sorry."

Tears spilled down her cheeks. "How did you know I was here? How did you get in? Do the nurses finally believe me?"

"I got away from your dad and then your stupid neighbor brought me here."

"Candice."

Macy nodded. "But it actually worked out because I wanted to help get you out of here."

"How'd you know I was here? If Dad wanted you to be me, he

wouldn't have told you I was here."

"I found your diaries."

"You read my private journals?" Heather's face flashed with anger. "How dare you?"

"How could I not? I didn't know what had happened to you or your mom. I knew nothing. You think Chester was going to tell me anything? Besides, I at least knew where to find you. That's why I didn't fight to get away from Candice. She was my ticket to get in here to help you get out."

Heather calmed down. "I probably would have done the same thing. Well, what about your family?"

"I need to get back to them after we get out of here. They have to be worried sick. I've been gone for months now."

"How are we going to get out? There are heavy, locked doors everywhere. You have to have a card to open them and the nurses don't leave those lying around. Trust me, I've looked."

"I have two ideas. Maybe together we can come up with more. But I thought we could either steal one of those cards to get out the doors or we can work to convince the nurses that you're cured."

Heather laughed. "Cured? There's nothing wrong with me. They're the jerks who won't listen to me. Dad has had everything covered, down to finding someone who sounds just like Mom to talk to everyone over the phone, pretending to be in Paris with her new love." She scowled. "I hate him so much. Anyway, that's why I'm so quick to believe that he replaced me with someone who looks exactly like me. Did you go to my school? Did my friends believe you?"

"He never let me out of the house. Can you think of another way to get us out?"

"It's going to take forever for them to believe that I've changed. I'm their trouble patient—and that's saying a lot around here. I just stopped caring. They wouldn't listen to me about Dad. He knows how to make people think what he wants."

"Do you think it's possible to sneak one of the key cards?"

"I've tried. They only ever keep those clipped onto the nurses' shirts."

"You don't think they have extras in that front desk somewhere?"

"They're not going to let us just walk up and go through the drawers."

"No, but they don't keep it manned all the time. When Candice brought me in, no one was there."

"Really? That's pretty rare. There must've been an incident. I've never seen it empty."

"What if we cause an incident? You act up and then I'll run to the desk when everyone is busy."

Heather looked like she was considering it. "The only problem with that is that if I act up, I'm going to solitary for a long, long time. What if they find both of us? Then they'd be forced to listen to us. I mean, really, if you've been kidnapped, they have to be able to find that out. They can pretend Mom's in Paris, but they can find out about you."

"Yeah, but then we're back to *you* being locked up here." Macy frowned.

"But you could tell them I'm not crazy. You've seen what Dad is capable of. If you tell them everything he did, they'll have no choice but to believe me and everything I've been saying all along. They'll know why I act out—because they won't listen to me. You'll get to go home, I'll get out of here, and Mom will finally get justice."

"Where will you go? Who will you stay with?"

"Either my grandparents or with my aunt and uncle. I guess it depends on who wants to take me. As long as I get out of here, I don't care."

"What do you think our best option is?" Macy asked.

"You know what? It would be fun to mess with the nurses and doctors here. After everything they've put me through, treating me worse than a criminal."

Macy groaned. "I just want to get home to my family. It's what, March? Your dad took me in November."

"Please help me mess with them. It's going to take us a while to get out of here anyway. We may as well have some fun."

"If we march out there together and tell them everything, they have to listen to us. The cops were just at your house this morning. Your dad is the one who needs to be taken care of—all of this is his fault. Everything he did to you and your mom, he needs to pay. He also needs to pay for kidnapping me. The staff here, they're nothing more than another one of his victims."

Heather snorted. "Trust me, girlfriend. They're not innocent. Come on, what's another day? We can screw with them and then tell them the truth after."

"And then have them pissed at us? They won't listen to us."

"You think they'll listen to us now? How long have you been here in my room posing as me? I was on the second floor all day. You know how to pretend to be me."

Macy put her face into her hands. Why was Heather being so difficult? She looked up and stared Heather in the eyes. "I've been pretending to be you for practically half a year. I just want to be me again and go home. I haven't seen my family in so long."

"At least you get to see yours." Tears shone in her eyes again. "My mom's dead and my dad's going to jail—not that I want to see him. I've had everything ripped from me, too, but when I leave here I'm not getting it back."

Macy's anger melted somewhat. "I'm sorry about that. I really am. But don't you want out of here? I want to *help* you get out. That's why I didn't fight Candice much when she tried to bring me here. I did try telling her I was kidnapped, but she wouldn't hear anything of it. She was convinced that I was you. Forget about getting back at them. Let's just try to get out of here. I know your grandparents would be more than happy to have you home with them. Think about them."

"How are they? I haven't seen them in, like, a year."

"Good. Ingrid taught me how to make some meals from scratch. She couldn't believe that you forgot."

A corner of Heather's mouth curled upward. "I'll bet. I've been cooking with her since I was little. Mom used to get so nervous with me so close to the stove. How's Grandpa?"

"Crotchety, but good."

"That sounds about right. Does he still bump heads with Dad all the time?"

"Yeah, they annoyed each other constantly."

"It would be good to see them." Heather ran her hands through her tangled hair. "I really would like to get back at the nurses, but you're right, it's not fair to you. You've had to deal with Dad all this time. So what are we going to do? Just walk out there together and say *listen to us?*"

Macy shrugged. "I've been trying to figure that out ever since I got here."

"I don't know if you noticed, but they locked us in. We either have to wait till morning or make a scene to get them in here. Then we have to hope they don't separate us."

"No one is going to check on you before morning?"

"Not unless I give them reason to."

"But it's a hospital. Aren't they supposed to check on you?"

Heather shook her head. "I'm locked inside with no way to get out. If I was on suicide watch or something, they'd have me in a room with a camera, but otherwise, nope. They just let us sleep and think."

Macy leaned her head against the wall. "I just want to get home."

"You may as well get comfortable. We can think up ideas before morning. Do you want the bed? I've slept in a padded room wearing a tight jacket. I can handle the floor."

"I've slept in the barn's cellar and in the back of your dad's truck. I can deal with the floor too."

Heather's eyes widened. "He put you in the storm cellar?"

"Until I agreed to call him Dad and answer to your name."

She looked like she was going to be sick. "I always wondered if he put Mom down there when she was missing. When she came back she kept saying the barn."

Macy remembered that from Heather's diaries, but wasn't going to say anything. "I did find a tube of lipstick down there."

Tears ran down Heather's face. "You know what? You're right. Screw the nurses. It's my dad we need to focus on." She got up and walked toward the door.

"Wait. What are you doing?"

"I'm going to pound on the door. With you here, they have to listen to me. They have to listen to *us.*"

"Hold on." Macy's heart raced so much she started to have trouble breathing. "Are you sure they'll listen to us? The last thing I want is to end up a patient here, too. They wouldn't send us to solitary? I don't want to be locked up anymore."

"We're already locked up, in case you haven't noticed."

"Yeah, but at least we're not alone. Do you know how long it's been since I've had someone to talk to? To actually plan something out with someone else?" It had been Luke three months earlier. "We'd better think this through."

Heather narrowed her eyes. "Why are you changing your mind all of a sudden?"

"Last time I acted rashly trying to escape, someone died."

"What the hell? Who?"

Macy went over to the bed and sat. "You'd better get comfortable. This is so crazy. You're going to want to sit."

Would Heather even believe that Chester had taken her to a cult's compound and had nearly risen to one of their top leaders?

Talking

A LYSSA ROLLED OVER in bed, feeling more refreshed than she had in a long time. The alarm clock next to the bed showed it was 8:37. How could she feel so refreshed after so little sleep? She had probably gone to bed after three, and it was probably after four by the time she fell asleep.

She stretched and realized she had to go the bathroom really bad. It was so bad that she was afraid she wouldn't make it across the hall. Alyssa scrambled out of bed, holding her breath. She barely made it.

Once she was washing her hands, she looked at herself in the mirror. She looked better—not back to normal, but better than she had in a while. The circles under her eyes had faded. She really felt rested too. It didn't make any sense.

How could she feel and look so much better after only a few hours of sleep?

Alyssa touched her face. It was oily. In fact, her hair felt the same way. On the inside, she felt great, but on the outside, she was gross. She needed a shower, especially since Rusty was bound to check on her soon.

She poked her head out the door to make sure he wasn't in sight and then she ran to the bedroom and grabbed her bag. She locked the bathroom and then got her supplies out of the bag, getting ready for a much needed shower.

Once Alyssa was cleaned up, she stepped out of the bathroom and the smell of bacon, eggs, and coffee greeted her. Her stomach rumbled.

Alyssa smiled as she threw her bag on the bed. Rusty was making *her* breakfast? Maybe she felt so rested because she was still asleep. No one cooked for her unless it was someone bringing the family dinner.

"Good morning," she said, announcing her presence as she walked into the kitchen.

Rusty turned around, wearing a red apron and holding a spatula. He smiled. "Did you sleep well?"

"I did, actually. I can't believe it's so early."

He gave her a funny look.

"What?"

"You slept for more than a day. You missed yesterday completely." He turned back to the stove, stirring something in a pan.

"I—you mean I slept over twenty-four hours?"

"Obviously you needed it. Have a seat. What do you take in your coffee?"

She sat down in the same chair she had sat in the night before. No, two nights before. "Creamer or milk and sugar. Whatever you have is fine. Not that I really need any after such a long sleep. Breakfast smells great. Can I help?"

"Nope. Let me take care of it. I'm almost done. It's nice to have someone else to cook for again."

Again? He was gorgeous and a cook? Lani had been one lucky lady. "I'm not going to complain about that."

"Glad to hear it." He used the spatula again and then moved over to the coffee maker.

As she watched him, her stomach growled again, and it was loud. Her face warmed up, hoping he couldn't hear it over the sizzling bacon. If he did, he didn't respond.

After a few minutes, he set a cup of coffee and a plate full of food in front of her. Alyssa's mouth watered. "That looks delicious."

Rusty sat down across from her with his own food. "I try, but don't rave about until after you eat it. Dig in. You must be starving after sleeping so long."

Looking at the food, she felt overwhelmed by everything. Why had he gone out of his way to take care of her? He hadn't had to tow her twice for free, bring her home, or cook this delicious meal. Voice cracking, she said, "Thank you."

He winked. "Again, not until you've tried it. Staring doesn't count."

She blinked back some tears. "No, really. I mean for everything. You haven't had to do anything for me, but you've done so much."

"People have helped me out also when I needed it. You know what they've asked me to do? Pay it forward. You're better than the decisions you've been making, Alyssa. I can see that much. I've been there, drowning in despair."

"That's it exactly."

"So eat now, before it gets cold. I want you to try it while it's still hot."

She cut a piece of the veggie filled, cheesy omelet. It nearly melted in her mouth.

Rusty looked at her expectantly.

Alyssa swallowed. "It's divine."

He smiled. "Perfect. Eat as much as you want. I made plenty. We'll probably warm it up and turn it into burritos later."

Later? How long was he expecting her to stay? Was he just being hospitable or did actually want her there? Not wanting to offend him or let the food get cold, she dug back in.

"Want more?" he asked as soon as she emptied her plate.

She did, but was afraid of stuffing herself. "I'm going to let it settle a little first." She picked up the coffee and brought it to her mouth. "Mmm. This is really good, too."

He grinned, his gorgeous eyes shining. "I do cook a mean breakfast, don't I?"

"That you do." She turned in her chair, blocking the bright morning sun shining on her face. It was going to be a beautiful Northwest spring day once the frost melted.

"Glad you like it, because I don't make much else unless I break out the grill."

"Do you grill all year?"

"Otherwise I'd eat out too much."

"In that case, I'll have to pay you back with a nice dinner."

"Sounds good to me." Rusty put his hands behind his head and looked at Alyssa.

They sat in a comfortable silence, sipping their coffees. Squinting, Alyssa looked outside at the back yard. As expected, there was a big play structure full of slides, swings, and climbers. His kids must have enjoyed it—and they probably thought they would have had many more years to enjoy it.

Tears filling her eyes, she turned to look at him. "How do you do it? Get through every day, I mean." The hole inside of her felt like it had been ripped even wider, knowing what he had gone through.

"Some days, that's all it is—getting through it. I would give anything for another day with them. Just one more hug." His face clouded over. "There are times I can't stand to be here. Other times, I can't leave. The memories are all I have aside from the things they left behind."

Alyssa wiped tears away. "That's exactly how I feel. As much as it kills me, I have to move on. I can't keep living like I've been."

He nodded, looking at something behind her. She turned around to see several children's drawings and paintings hanging on the wall.

She turned around. "It's so unfair."

A tear ran down Rusty's face. "That it is. But on the other hand, I'm grateful for the time with them I did have. I wouldn't give that up for anything, even though the pain sometimes feels like it's going to kill me."

"It's never going to go away, is it?" asked Alyssa.

He wiped his cheek. "It gets better, but it also gets worse. I don't think it ever disappears. At least I hope not. I don't want to forget. Somehow the pain helps to keep the other emotions alive, too."

Alyssa raised an eyebrow.

"It does get easier to a degree, as I'm sure you've found. First, there's the initial horror followed by the stages of grief until we hit acceptance."

She nodded. "That's where I'm at. I think. But it gets worse?"

"I went through hell on the first anniversary of crash. I nearly went back to the booze, but the thought of going back to rehab was enough to keep me away. That and knowing none of them would want me to turn into a drunk. I nearly lost the house when I was in rehab—the very house where my kids lived their entire lives." Be blinked fast for a moment. "I used that as my anchor to keep everything together. That was when I decided to go into towing with the primary aim of keeping drunks off the road. I couldn't save my family, but maybe I could save someone else's."

Alyssa nodded, afraid of her voice. If she spoke, she might end up a sobbing mess.

"Then I joined a grief group. I'm not sure if it helped, but I couldn't keep going." His lips curled down. "There were too many people there who didn't want to move on. That wasn't what I wanted."

"The therapist didn't try to move the focus?"

"It was just a group. I think if it had a counselor of some kind, that would have helped. It was run by people who wanted to connect with other grieving people. That was probably part of the problem. That and the fact that the ones who were stuck tended to dominate things. I couldn't deal with it."

Taking another sip, Alyssa nodded. They sat quietly again for a while. She looked at the framed paintings on the walls and thought those—and everything else in the house—must be reminders of Lani and the boys. How did he do it?

She at least still had Chad and Alex. What would she have done if she had lost all three of them? There was no way she would have held it together as well as Rusty had. She cleared her throat. "Last night when I was lying in bed, I spoke to Macy. I felt a lot better. Actually, I think that's why I was able to sleep so well."

Rusty sniffled, giving her a sad look. "They still haven't found anything?"

Alyssa played with her hands under the table. "No. I don't know what the holdup is. I'm sick of it though. I just want answers. That's what Chad and I have been fighting about. I don't see how she can still be alive after all this time. It's time to move on and accept she's not coming back. Do you think I'm a horrible person? Do you think I'm giving up?"

"No, you're not horrible for giving up. I'm in no position to judge. I never had to live with the unknown. Reality was forced upon me from the moment it happened."

"I don't *want* her be dead," Alyssa said, her voice high. "That's the last thing I want, but I don't see how there's another possible outcome. Even if that one girl isn't her, we still know nothing about Macy. She's gone and she's not coming back. I can't keep acting like she is." The tears came again and Alyssa knew she was going to lose control.

She put her forehead on the table and sobbed. She was vaguely aware of Rusty sitting next to her and putting his arm around her. He didn't say anything. After what felt like forever, she looked up at Rusty, knowing she looked like crap and also not caring. "I'm not a bad mother. I'm not. I just have to face the facts."

"You don't have to explain yourself to me. You've gotta do what you think is right."

Why couldn't Chad be this understanding? She crumpled, aware of the table coming at her face but not caring enough to do anything about it. She felt hands grasp her and found her head against Rusty's chest. He held onto her tightly.

"You're safe here. Just let it all out. Scream, cry or whatever you need to."

She closed her eyes, giving into the sobs once again. Screaming sounded nice, but she didn't have it in her then. She would have to do that another time. Alyssa felt drowsy, unable to open her eyes as she cried and shook. She really did feel safe.

Feelings

ALYSSA OPENED HER eyes trying to figure out where she was. It took a moment to realize she was in Rusty's guest room. How had she gotten there? The last thing she remembered was sobbing against his chest.

She smelled something cooking. Was that what had woken her up? She stretched and thought about what to do. Part of her wanted to stay in bed and never get up again, but that wouldn't solve anything. On the other hand, she wasn't sure how she felt about getting up to face Rusty after turning into an emotional mess like that.

Closing her eyes, she pretended that she was a careless teenager sleeping in a weekend. She had been able to out-sleep anyone back then.

The smell of food grew stronger and her stomach rumbled. She grabbed her bag and went into the bathroom. She looked as bad as she had suspected. She brushed her hair, but that didn't help, so she pulled it back into a simple ponytail before putting on some eye makeup and lip color. Nothing too fancy, but enough to look human again.

She got a flashback of teaching Macy how to put on makeup. At only twelve, she wanted to be grown up. Alyssa had been excited to show her how to put it on, even though she knew Chad would throw a fit—which he had, of course, since he didn't want Macy growing up.

Alyssa threw her eyeliner in the bag. Now he had his wish.

Not wanting to think about him any longer, she stormed into the guest room and threw her bag on the bed. Alyssa had to calm down before going into the kitchen. Rusty didn't deserve her anger, nor did she want to talk about Chad with him.

She made the bed and then paced the room, trying to calm herself.

When she felt halfway normal, she decided to go to the kitchen. Maybe helping him with dinner would get her mind off everything. It smelled like he was making those omelet burritos he had mentioned earlier.

Tightening her fists, Alyssa took several deep breaths. She still felt anger burning toward Chad deep in her gut, but she would have to ignore that. At least she had someone to talk with who understood her.

She opened the door and went into the kitchen. Rusty had his back to her, cooking over the stove again. Alyssa walked over to him. "Do you want some help with that?"

He jumped. "You startled me. Did you get enough rest?"

"I suppose so. I can't remember going back to bed."

"You wouldn't. You fell asleep out here and I carried you back there."

"Sorry. Usually I'm not so lazy."

"You're not. Clearly your body needs rest. I have a feeling it's not something you've given yourself much of in a while."

"Not for lack of trying."

"Sometimes a new environment can make all the difference. I did the same thing when I went to rehab. If they would've let me, I would have slept for a week. Here, can you stir this?" He handed her a wooden spoon.

"Sure."

He grabbed some tortillas and salsa and somehow turned their break-fast into a respectable dinner.

"I thought you could only make breakfast and use a barbecue."

Rusty shrugged. "Maybe I exaggerated a little."

Alyssa actually smiled.

He pointed to a little pot at the back of the stove. "Can you stir those, please?"

She picked up another spoon and stirred, getting the refried beans unstuck from the bottom.

"Add some of this." He handed her a jar of sauce.

"What's this?" She looked at the blank jar.

"My special ingredient."

"Okay." She sprinkled a little on and stirred again.

"You'll need more of that."

She dumped a bunch in.

"Easy there. Not so much."

Alyssa smiled. "Make up your mind." She forgot about her problems as they finished making the burritos, even laughing and teasing each other. By the time they sat down to eat, she felt better than she had in a long time. Maybe a change of scenery—and people—was exactly what she needed.

When they were done eating, Rusty gathered the dishes and put them into the sink. He turned on the water and Alyssa stood up. "Don't even think about it. I'm going to clean those."

He moved aside. "Be my guest. I'll be right back."

She washed the dishes, ignoring the dishwasher. She scrubbed away her frustrations on the dishes, pots, and pans. When she was done, she went to the living and found Rusty putting on his coat.

"Grab your coat. We're going on a walk," he said.

"We are?"

"You need some fresh air. Hurry up. I'm not going to wait forever." The skin around his eyes wrinkled, indicating that he was holding back a smile.

"Yes, sir." She went back to the guest room and grabbed her coat, putting it on as she headed for the living room. The front door was open and Rusty was nowhere to be seen. Alyssa peeked outside and saw him standing on the porch, looking at the sky. The sun was going down and it was colored in pinks and oranges.

She stepped outside. "It's beautiful."

He nodded, still looking at it. "Nothing like sunsets around here." He closed and locked the door. "We'd better hurry before it gets dark."

"Are we going anywhere in particular?"

"There's a trail not too far away. It's peaceful and helps me to stay centered."

"Sounds nice." She followed him, trying to stay at his side. They walked in silence as she took in the beauty of the tall, dark green pine trees surrounding them with the sunset framing them. Soon they were walking along a dirt trail. Squirrels scampered along the ground, chattering at each other. She heard a stream somewhere and with it, the occasional frog calling out.

They came to a fork in the trail and they went left. The sound of the stream grew louder and he stopped in front of a row of benches. He sat down without a word and Alyssa sat on the same bench, but not too close. She looked around at the scenery, her eyes resting on the sky, its hues darker.

She breathed in the fresh air, noticing the spring scents of new life. Even the dirt smelled sweet. A flock of noisy geese flew overhead in a V-shape. She ran her hands through her ponytail, noticing that her body felt relaxed.

Then it hit her. Alyssa hadn't thought of Macy the entire walk. She hadn't once thought of her dead daughter. She was a horrible parent. Wasn't she supposed to take Macy with her wherever she went?

"Are you okay?" Rusty asked.

She turned to look at Rusty, unable to admit the truth. She just stared at him, finding it hard to focus on the details of his face because it was getting dark.

"Alyssa?"

Would he understand? Or would he think she was as horrible as she felt?

"What's the matter? Remember, I've been through this too."

"I forgot about her."

"You forgot...?"

"Macy. I didn't think about her the entire time we've been out here." Alyssa expected tears, but those were missing too.

Rusty nodded, probably having a knowing look on his face. "It's a normal part of moving on. I remember the first time I noticed that too. I felt terrible, but we can't hang onto them every moment. We didn't before. Even when they were with us, there were times we lived and didn't think about them."

"I don't know how I feel about this. I don't want to forget. I want to move on, but..."

"You're not forgetting her. Actually, you're in the acceptance stage. That's part of it."

The tears finally came. "I don't want to accept it. It doesn't feel right. It..." She wiped the tears, feeling like a jumbled mess.

He scooted over and sat about an inch away. "It's okay to feel whatever you feel. Feelings simply are. They're not right or wrong. I've been through all of this."

She leaned her head against his shoulder. "I felt normal again. It was wonderful, but horrible at the same time."

"That's nothing to feel guilty about. We can't go through life mourning forever. We would end up depressed and eventually suicidal. Our families wouldn't want that, would they?"

"No. I remember times when I was upset, and Macy hated that. She always tried to cheer me up." More tears filled her eyes. Even though it was nearly dark, she tried to blink them away.

"See? She would want you having times like this—enjoying life."

Alyssa's throat made an awful noise as the tears fell onto her face. She gave into the sob, determined not to turn into a blubbering mess this time.

Rusty put his arm around her. She imagined Macy telling her to move on. As guilty as she felt, she knew that was what she had to do. It wasn't good for her and it wasn't any good for Alex, either. He needed her to be strong.

The air suddenly felt cold and she shivered, leaning closer to Rusty.

"Are you ready to get back?"

"Not really, but we probably should. Hopefully we can see the path."

Rusty pulled something out from his jacket. She heard a click and then saw a light. He was holding a huge flashlight. "This will make sure that we do." He stood and held his hand out.

Alyssa took it and stood.

He let go and started walking. "Let yourself relax and think about nothing. It's good for you."

"All right." Alyssa said a silent apology to Macy and then focused on what she could see in the light.

They walked the rest of the way back to his house in silence. The stars were bright and beautiful and the moon was off to the side, only a small sliver. There were a few clouds, but it was a mostly clear night.

When they reached the house, Alyssa found herself wanting to stay outside. There was a swing on his porch, so she sat.

"Do you want to sit by yourself or would like company?" asked Rusty.

"You can stay. Or if you have to get to work, you can go. I don't want to keep you from anything."

"No. I'll go out later." He sat down.

She looked at him, this time able to see him better thanks to the porch light. One curl hung right over his forehead. She wanted to brush it away.

He leaned back into the swing. "Even though it was hard, I'm glad you went for the walk. There's something about nature that helps bring us where we need to be. At least it works that way with me."

"Me, too. Thank you, Rusty."

"It's nothing."

"Nothing? It's everything. You can't imagine how much you've helped."

"I've just given you a chance to get away from everything. You can stay as long as you need to—I mean that. Consider the room yours. Even when you go back home and need to get away, please come here rather than the bar. I don't want to find you there again."

Swallowing, she looked into his eyes. Before she knew what was happening, she leaned over and placed her lips on top of his. He smelled of aftershave and dinner.

He pulled back. "I'm sorry if I gave you the wrong impression. I was only—"

"Oh my gosh. I can't believe I just did that." Her face heated up. Of course he wouldn't find her attractive. He was off the charts handsome and she was a hot mess—all the time. He had driven her home twice because she was drunk. Just like the person who had killed his family. "I'll go now." She ran for the door, but it was locked.

Rusty got up and moved her hands from the door, giving her a kind look. "Don't be embarrassed. You're beautiful, Alyssa, but you're also grieving. If I allowed anything to happen, I would be taking advantage of you. Not only that, but you're married."

"Just let me inside."

He put his hand on her shoulder. "Do you know what I would give for one more day with my wife? You have that opportunity with Chad. Take all the time you need to work through your feelings here. I'm your *friend,* but what I really want is to see you back with your family."

Alyssa sighed and leaned against the door.

Returning

ALYSSA TURNED THE lock on her front door, holding her breath. Would Chad and Alex be angry with her or happy to see her? She hadn't even told Alex she was going anywhere, and she had been gone a couple of days. She was only there to get some more clothes and talk with Alex. With any luck, she would be able to avoid Chad. If he was working on his blog, she might actually be able to stay off his radar.

She walked in and closed the door behind her.

Alex appeared at the top of the stairs. "Mom."

Alyssa couldn't tell if he was happy to see her or upset.

"Oh, baby. I'm sorry I took off like I did." She went up the stairs, trying to read his face. He didn't give her any clues. She wrapped her arms around him and he returned the hug, squeezing tight.

"I was worried, but Dad said you needed some time to think about everything."

Alyssa nodded, stepping back. "He's right. You were already asleep when I realized I needed some space to think." If Chad hadn't mentioned their fight, neither would she.

"Are you staying?" he asked.

She tousled his hair. "I'm going to stay with a friend for a little while. But if you need me, call."

"Why didn't you answer your phone? It kept going to voice mail."

"I didn't bring my charger with me, but this time I will. I'm really sorry, Alex. How have you been doing the last couple of days?"

He shrugged, looking annoyed. "Dad's been on his computer non-stop, and Zoey isn't feeling well."

"Is she okay?"

"I guess. Her back's hurting and she's tired a lot."

"Do you want to grab some ice cream? It would be nice to sit and talk."

"We don't have any."

"Let's go out and get some. It'll do you good to get out of the house. It's helped me a lot."

"Not enough to stay here. I'm getting ready for bed, actually. Zoey's appointment is in the morning and I'm going with her this time."

Alyssa gave him another hug. "Let's plan to do something. I miss you."

"Are you moving out?"

"Honestly, I don't know. I'm not looking that far ahead. I need some time."

"To get away from Dad? I thought you guys were getting along."

She bit her lip. "We just need to work things out."

"What's to work out? We need you here. Not at Sharon's house or wherever you've been. Why didn't you call? Is there no phone there?"

Alyssa should have known that he would be upset. "I slept all of yesterday, sweetie. As in, I didn't even wake up once. I'll call you tomorrow, I promise. I want to hear about the appointment. And then maybe we can get some lunch."

"Whatever. 'Night, Mom." He turned around, but before he could walk away, Alyssa grabbed him and gave him a big hug.

"I really have missed you, Alex."

He hugged her back. "I know. Me too, Mom." Alex went up the stairs and down the hall and toward his room. Alyssa could hear him close the door behind him.

The last thing she needed was to lose him, too. He was right there. If she messed things up with him, then she really was an awful mom. She would need to get herself together so she could come home soon.

What if Chad continued to insist that Macy was still alive out there? If he held onto that fantasy, insisting that Alyssa did too, there was no way she could stay at home.

As much as it had ripped her apart out in the woods, moving on was what she needed. She couldn't hold onto the hope of Macy's return. Even though she wanted nothing more, she knew her daughter wasn't going to be back. All she could cling to was the hope that Macy hadn't suffered.

She needed to get to the place where Rusty was—somehow able to feel blessed that he had had the time he did with his family. Realizing that she had been standing in the same spot for a few minutes, she went up the stairs and thought about what she was going to pack. Mostly just clothes; she had already packed the other stuff she needed.

When she walked into her room, Chad was sitting on the bed. His back was to her, but she could see the glow from his phone. It sounded like he was texting.

She cleared her throat.

He turned around and looked surprised, hopeful even. "Are you staying?" he asked.

She shook her head. "I need some more clothes."

"You look good. Have you gotten some sleep finally?"

"That's almost all I've done. I missed yesterday entirely, actually."

"That explains why we haven't heard from you."

She went into the closet and grabbed some clothes from their hangers.

Chad's arms wrapped around her shoulders, pulling her into him. Her entire body tensed. She held her clothes close to her stomach.

He took a deep breath. "You smell like the outdoors."

"I went for a walk before coming here."

"Won't you stay? I've missed you so much. So has Alex. He—"

"I've already talked with him."

"What can I do to convince you to stay?"

She turned around, staring him down. "We can't agree to disagree. That works for some things, Chad, but not this. We have to accept the facts and move on. I can't do that if you refuse. We're living in two different realities."

He frowned. "You really want to give her a funeral?"

"She deserves it."

"What will we tell her when she returns? That we gave up on her?"

Alyssa pursed her lips, anger burning. "I'm not giving up on my daughter. I'm accepting the facts. It's what she would have wanted us to do. She wouldn't have wanted us to live like this."

Chad took a long, deep breath. "What if we agree to wait for the DNA results?"

"That could be another three months. Maybe longer the way they move. I can't keep my life on hold. I may sound like a horrible person, but I need closure."

"Are you moving out?"

"I'm giving myself space to heal. If you would give that to me, we can discuss my staying here. I can't move on if you don't."

"I can't give up on her. But I don't want you to leave, either."

"Then it looks like we have a stalemate." She turned around and grabbed more clothes, not even paying attention to what she was taking. She just made sure not to take any summer dresses.

When her arms were full, she threw the clothes onto the bed and went back into the closet and found her largest suitcase.

"We can make this work, Lyss." Chad begged her with his eyes.

She threw the luggage onto the bed. "No, we can't." She piled the clothes in, not bothering to fold them. "I can't do this. Not anymore. We've been together our entire lives and I'm sorry that it's come down to this, but we're obviously not made for each other anymore."

"What will Macy think when she comes home to find you gone?"

"She's not coming home! Don't you get that? She's never going to be back." She slammed the suitcase shut and zipped it, fighting tears.

"Alex needs you. I need you."

"Don't pull a guilt trip on me. If you really want to make this work, you'll pull your head out of your butt and face reality. Until then, I can't be here." She lifted the baggage with grunt.

"Let me help you with that."

"Stop! Just leave me alone." She put it on the floor and wheeled it out of the room.

"Where are you staying?"

"With a friend. Don't worry, I'll bring my charger."

"How can you do this?"

Alyssa turned around. "How can I do this? If you have to ask, you really don't get it. I'll see you later." She stopped in front of Alex's door. "Honey, I'm leaving. I'll call you tomorrow."

"Okay," came Alex's voice from the other side of the door.

She waited a moment and realized with a stinging sensation that he wasn't going to come out. "Talk to you then. I love you."

He said something, but it was too muffled to understand.

"You won't stay even for him?" Chad asked, still behind her.

"Not if you're going to be here. I can't handle it. Getting away was the best thing I've done for myself. You can think I'm selfish if you want. I really don't care anymore. Like I've already said too many times, this isn't something we can agree to disagree about."

A pressing weight pushed against her on all sides. She needed to get out of the house even though it was probably going to be awkward around Rusty after having kissed him. Looking at Chad, she knew she should feel guilty about it, but she didn't need any more guilt in her life. If anything, he had pushed her away—right to Rusty.

Alyssa looked around the hall, everything reminding her of Macy. There was no way she could stay there and move on with so many memories. Maybe she could come back after she had a chance to heal—if that ever happened. Could she get to the place where Rusty was? He was functioning and living a productive life in the same house that his family had lived in.

Chad looked at her. "Are you thinking about staying?"

"No. Maybe if we were on the same page, but even then, I don't know. It would be a start, at least." She yanked on the suitcase and went down the stairs with it. Somehow she managed to get it in the car without any tears or arguments.

As she drove away, the suffocation released its hold. It let go all the more as she got farther away. By the time she pulled back into Rusty's driveway, she felt human again. The tow truck was gone, which meant that he wasn't there. After the earlier embarrassment, it was a relief.

She obviously needed some space from him to think about everything. Getting away to talk with Alex the next day would help also. Exhaustion hit her and she was glad to be able to go in and just sleep. She took the key out of the ignition and then checked for the key Rusty had given her.

When she got inside, she went straight for the guest room and barely took the time to get into her pajamas before climbing into bed. She had another conversation with Macy, explaining why she had to stay at Rusty's instead of at home. Macy would understand.

Then Alyssa remembered to plug in her phone. She turned it on and scrolled through the missed calls and texts. There were quite a few from Alex and Chad over the last couple of days.

She went over to the gallery of pictures and the one it opened up to—the last one she had taken—was Macy smiling at her. She was holding Ducky. It was shortly after Macy had gotten the little black and white ferret. Smiling, Alyssa scrolled through the pictures, stopping at each one of Macy.

Some of them she couldn't even remember taking. It was like seeing them for the first time. It was a gift from Macy just when she needed it most. Alyssa scrolled through the pictures until her vision was too blurry. She blinked away the tears, turned the phone on silent, and went to sleep.

Demands

C HAD WOKE WITH a start, having rolled onto Alyssa's empty side of the bed.

They had been getting along so well over the last few months, it was still a shock to have her gone, mad at him. As much as he wanted to her to stay, he wasn't going to give in and have a memorial service for their daughter who was still alive. He couldn't explain it, and that was part of the problem, but he had a feeling that Macy was alive out there somewhere.

It was a feeling that he had learned not to ignore. It was actually the same one that he had had when he met Alyssa back in high school. He knew she was the one. Even though he was young—about Macy's age, maybe a little older; it was hard to remember the little details over twenty years later—he knew without a doubt that Alyssa was the girl for him. He *knew* they were going to get married and have a family together.

He had been right about that, and he was right about this too. That meant that even though it upset Alyssa, he wasn't going to give in and admit defeat. If somehow the DNA results showed that the girl in the morgue was his daughter, then he would have to give in and face those facts, but he knew that wouldn't happen.

Why was it taking so long to get those results? After nearly four months, he would have expected something. With technology as it was, they should have been able to get what they needed.

Chad rolled to the other side of the bed and checked his phone. Alyssa hadn't called. Hopefully that meant she had spent the evening talking with Sharon and gotten some much-needed sleep.

He needed to get up and check the blog comments and write a new post, but he knew he wasn't in any state of mind to focus on that. It would be half-hearted at best and he couldn't do that. If he had to get a late start, so be it.

What he needed to do was go down to the police station—not just call—and pester them until he got answers that he could live with. He had been patient long enough. Now it was time to put pressure on them.

Maybe that was the problem. He had just done everything the cops told them to do. Now it was time to say no.

He took a quick shower before heading to the kitchen. It startled him to see Alex and Zoey sitting at the table. They were eating cold cereal and had their school work out.

"Up so early?"

"My appointment is today," Zoey said.

"Oh, right. It's hard to believe you'll already find out the sex. What do you guys think it'll be?"

Alex looked up, pale.

Zoey shrugged her shoulders, taking a bite of rainbow-colored food.

"No ideas? I thought the moms always had a feeling."

"Not me."

Chad stared at Alex. "You okay, son?"

Alex sat up. "I'm great, Dad. Couldn't be better."

"Hey, I need to show you something." He turned to Zoey. "Mind if I borrow him for a minute?"

"Sure. I gotta get this assignment turned in before we go anyway." She turned to her laptop.

"Perfect. Come on, Alex." Chad went upstairs to the bonus room and sat on the couch.

Alex sat next to him. "What do you need to show me in here?"

"Nothing. I just want to talk to you alone."

"What is it? I have homework to turn in too."

"I want to make sure you're okay."

"I told you down there. I'm fine."

Chad tilted his head and gave Alex a knowing look, the same look his own dad used to give him when he was alive.

Alex scowled. "Okay. I'm not fine. I feel like I'm going to puke. Happy?"

"Of course not. Is there anything I can do?"

"Like what?"

Good question. Alyssa was always the one who knew what to do when it came to the kids. "Do you want me to go with you to the appointment? I can skip my blog post today."

"You would do that for me?"

He put his hand on Alex's shoulder. "Of course."

Alex gave him a strange look. "Thanks, but I'm going with Zoey and her mom."

Chad sighed, relieved. Seeing an ultrasound was too much reality for him. Maybe that was giving Alex anxiety. "Are you worried about seeing the baby?"

Alex looked away. "I dunno."

"I'll never forget when I first saw your sister and you on the screen. It was amazing and terrifying at the same time."

"Really?" Alex turned to him, looking somewhat relieved himself. "You felt that way? Both times?"

Chad nodded.

"But weren't you ready for it the second time?"

"Nope. Both times, it freaked me out. I can't tell you how scared I was that I would be in charge of someone's life. I kept a calm face for your mom because she needed my support, but inside I was freaking out."

"How did you deal with it?"

"I went out with the guys and had some beer. Obviously, you can't do that, but we can have some guy time tonight. We could hit the arcade."

Alex looked like he was considering it. "If you'll buy me the unlimited pass."

That was expensive and he had always told Alex he could get the pass one day. "Sure. Today's the day I get it for you. We'll play until you don't want to see another video game again."

"Or until they close."

"Whichever comes first."

"Deal. Thanks, Dad." Alex gave him a hug, surprising Chad.

He hugged Alex back. "My pleasure. I've got some errands to take care of today, so if I'm not here when you get back, I won't be long."

"Okay." Alex left the room.

Chad couldn't help smiling. He had actually handled that pretty well. Alyssa would have been proud, even though she wouldn't have liked Alex playing arcade games for hours on end. The kid deserved it. Chad remembered the stress and reality that those sonograms brought. He couldn't begin to imagine dealing with it at thirteen.

Besides, Alyssa wasn't even there. If she wanted to be involved in these decisions, she shouldn't have run off to her friend's place.

His stomach rumbled and he went back downstairs. The kids were busy on their computers, so he didn't bother them. He grabbed some frozen pancakes and stuck them in the microwave. After eating, he said a quick goodbye and then got in the car, thinking about what he would say to the cops.

Their shifts varied, so he didn't even know if he would be able to talk to the ones he had been working with since Macy disappeared. Even if they were off duty, he would put some pressure on whoever was there.

Chad marched into the station like he belonged there. He ignored the people sitting in the waiting room and walked straight to the front desk.

"Is Detective Fleshman here?"

"He's off duty. Can I help you?"

"How about Officers Anderson or Reynolds?"

"I believe Officer Reynolds is still here. He had a bunch of paperwork after his last—wait a minute. You are?"

"Chad Mercer. They're working with me on the case of my missing daughter."

Recognition washed over his face. "Oh, right. They're still looking for her?"

Chad could hear hushed conversation behind him. "Yes, of course. Will you tell Reynolds that I need to speak with him?"

"Have a seat."

"I'll just stand here." Chad stepped back, keeping watch on the desk.

"Whatever. I'll let him know you're here." The officer got up and disappeared behind a wall.

Chad pulled out his phone and scrolled through his apps, pretending to be involved in a texting conversation. He was all too aware of the stares and whispers. Unfortunately, it had become a regular part of life outside the house. Couldn't people understand he was just a regular guy who happened to have a missing daughter? He was normal, just like them, except for the fact that his heart had been ripped out of his chest and stomped on while the world watched.

"Reynolds will see you. You know where room six is?"

Chad put his phone in his pocket and nodded. He knew where the rooms were and he could find number six since they were all labeled. He went around the desk and down the hall. He would have been happy to have gone his whole life without ever seeing those walls.

He found door number six and went in. It was empty. He paced back and forth before walking around the table several times. He was more than aware of the *mirror* on the back wall. He was tempted to wave or make a face at whoever might be watching him. Didn't they have rooms without the two-way mirrors for non-criminals?

Tired of walking around, he pulled a chair out and sat down. After a few minutes, Officer Reynolds walked in, wearing his signature hat. "Hey, Chad. I hope you weren't waiting too long. Paperwork is my least favorite part of the job."

"What's going on with the DNA testing?"

"They've yet to get a viable sample." Reynolds sat across from Chad.

"I know that much. What is anyone doing to get one?"

"If the latest test yields nothing, they're going to send her out of state to a more sophisticated lab."

"I knew that, too. More needs to be done. Since they've had such a challenging time getting a good sample, why don't they take more? Run five at a time. Do something."

Reynolds set his hat on the table and looked into Chad's eyes. "We're doing all we can. There are other cases and they can't be ignored."

"Is Macy's case getting pushed back?"

"No. If it wasn't important, they would drop it. It's still a missing child case and that's why it's going outside of the state after this. Macy is still a priority."

"I just want to make sure."

"We haven't moved on."

Chad narrowed his eyes. "I still say more needs to be done."

Meeting

ZOEY PACED HER room, looking out the window every five seconds. Despite all of her protests, she was about to meet her dad—no, her sperm donor. That's all he was. Nothing more. She would take a look into his eyes and see where she got the majority of her looks. She did look like her mom, not that anyone ever noticed because of her coloring.

She looked out the window again. Where were they? Her mom had texted her that they were on their way. Maybe there was traffic. Hopefully they were arguing. That way her mom would make him stay somewhere else.

How dare she invite him to live with them? Neither one of them knew the man. Sure, she had slept with him for a while. Maybe she had even wanted to get pregnant. She always prided herself on being a strong single mom and she knew he was going back to Japan.

Maybe Zoey's anger had been misplaced. Her mom might have been the one who had decided that Zoey didn't need a dad. Who was she to decide that? Just because she didn't want to deal with a husband, and that was incredibly selfish.

She looked around the room and stopped when she saw a small jewelry box her mom had given her years ago. Zoey walked over to it and held it up to the light, looking at the intricate designs. Then she clutched it in her hand and threw it on the hardwood floor, watching it smash into dozens of pieces.

Instead of chewing the sperm donor out, she was going to let them both have it. They had both agreed to the stupid, selfish plan. Did either of them give even one thought to Zoey and what she would have wanted? It didn't look that way. One wanted to get halfway across the world to hit a ball and the other wanted to be the sole decision maker in Zoey's life.

She picked up the last birthday card her mom had given her and ripped into tiny pieces, letting them fall on the floor next to the jewelry box pieces.

Zoey was glad that she had been smoking before getting pregnant—it hit her mom where it hurt. Just like she deserved. Even though Zoey had been dealing with horribly painful headaches among other things since quitting, she was glad she told her mom about her smoking. The look on her face had been worth it.

She was even happier to have gotten pregnant. That hit them both where it hurt. She was sure that neither of them wanted to be grandparents at their age. It was too bad she couldn't do more to make them pay. Although having a pregnant fifteen year old daughter was a pretty good hit.

Zoey heard a car pull into the driveway. The moment of truth was about to arrive. She went to her window and looked down. Sure enough, there was her mom's car with someone in the passenger seat next to her. He even appeared to be wearing a baseball cap. How fitting. Too bad the jerk couldn't play anymore. Then Zoey wouldn't have to deal with him at all.

Should she go down and meet them, or should she make them come up to get her? Zoey looked at the mess on the floor and didn't want to deal with a lecture. Not that she cared if her mom saw what she had broken. Let her, so it would hurt.

Zoey stepped over the mess and made her way down the stairs as slowly as possible. She could hear something downstairs by the door.

"Is that you, Zo?" called her mom.

"No. It's a burglar."

Her mom muttered something, but Zoey was too far away to hear. "Hurry up. Your dad's excited to meet you."

Zoey bit her tongue. There was so much wrong with that sentence she didn't even know where to begin. "Coming." She didn't pick up her pace. She took her time making her way to them. Before she rounded the corner, she flattened her shirt so that her stomach stuck out as much as possible. Usually, she wore the loosest clothing possible, but not today.

She wanted her *dad* to have a good view.

She turned down the hall and walked to the entry, trying not to look at him, but curiosity made her want to look. How much did she look like him? Zoey kept her focus on her mom. "Are we ready for the appointment?"

Valerie scowled. "You have time to meet your dad." She turned to him. "Zoey, this is your dad. Kenji, this is Zoey."

Zoey glanced at him and gave a slight nod of the head. "Hi." She turned back to her mom. "Are we ready? We need to get Alex."

"Would you stop being rude? Give him a proper greeting?"

A proper welcome? Zoey turned to him. She tried to look past him, not taking in his features. "Hi, Kenji. Thanks for not being in my life. It's been awesome."

He opened his mouth, but Valerie spoke up first.

"Zoey!" She turned to Kenji. "I'm so sorry. I knew she might be in a mood, but I didn't expect this."

"Then I guess you don't know me very well, do you? I'm going to get Alex."

"Alex? Wait, we talked about this."

"No, Mom. You talked about it, but you didn't listen to me. Alex is coming with me. He hasn't been to any of my appointments. He deserves to be at this one. You know, he's been involved this whole time."

Kenji made eye contact with Zoey. "I understand this is hard for you. It's going to take time. I should have been involved, but I thought it was best if I didn't. We both did." He looked at Valerie. "I do care about you and hope you'll give me a chance. If you don't want to for a while, I respect that."

"Kenji, don't. She needs to—"

"This is a big adjustment and she has every right to be angry." He turned to look her in the eyes. "If you feel the need to—what the expression?—tell me off, you're more than welcome. Anything you need to say to me is good. Then I hope we can move past it and get to know each other."

Zoey stared at him, feeling deflated. If he knew he deserved to be ripped into, it was going to take half the pleasure out of it. "Maybe I'll take you up on that. I'm going to get Alex. See you in the car."

"Why don't you help us unload the rest of his stuff?" Valerie asked.

"Nope. I'm going to get Alex."

Her mom looked like she was going to explode. Good.

"She's fine," Kenji said.

"No, she's not! Zoey, you better—"

"Zoey, go get your boyfriend. I'll take care of my luggage."

"See you in the car." Zoey walked past them and out the door. Once the door closed behind her, she found herself shaking. She tried to stop, but couldn't. Why not? He was just some guy from the other side of the planet. Nothing to get worked up over. He was just another random stranger. Nothing more.

She took a deep breath and then made her way over to Alex's house. The driveway was empty. Did that mean neither of his parents were home? Not that it mattered. There were enough parents at her house to make up for the whole street.

The front door opened before she even got there. Alex closed it behind him. "Are we ready?"

"Yeah. My mom and sperm donor arrived just in time. I don't know how my mom does it. She always knows how to plan everything perfectly."

"So, what's he like?"

"Who knows? I barely said hi to him before coming to get you."

"Really? I know you're pissed, but aren't you curious?"

"Not really. Let's go. I want to find out if the baby's a boy or a girl. I'm tired of everyone calling it *it*."

"Okay." He looked like he wanted to say more, but he took her hand. "I want to know what it is, too."

Alex took her hand they walked to her house in silence. Zoey stopped when they got to her mom's car.

"We're not going in the house?"

"I told them we'd meet them in the car."

"Okay." He opened the back door and waited for Zoey to go in first. They settled in. "Is he nice, at least?"

Zoey shrugged. "He said I could chew him out if I wanted."

"Are you going to?"

"Probably, though it takes half the fun out of it since he said that."

"Fun?"

"You know what I mean. Not like ha-ha fun, but it'll feel good to let him have it. But if he's nice and not a jerk, it won't be the same. I wanted him to be mean. He said he was wrong and seemed to believe it. Said he thought keeping his distance was for the best."

He bumped her. "You're not half-bad, so he can't be too bad."

Zoey gave him a light shove and glared at him.

Alex laughed and then the corners of Zoey's mouth twitched. "Don't try to make me feel better."

"I'm just sayin'. I like you."

"Really? I would have never guessed."

He feigned a hurt expression and they both laughed. "At least you're smiling now."

"We'll see how long that lasts."

Alex looked toward the front of the house.

"Are they coming?" Zoey asked.

"Yeah. I'm trying to get a good look at your dad."

"Sperm donor," Zoey corrected.

"He looks a lot like you. Like, it's obvious he's your dad."

Zoey rolled her eyes. "I'm supposed to care?"

"Maybe you should give him a chance."

"And maybe you should back off."

Zoey's *parents* came to the car and Kenji introduced himself to Alex. It looked like Alex was going to pee himself. Was he nervous about meeting her sperm donor?

"Hi, sir. It's nice to meet you." Alex held out his hand between the front seats.

"Good to meet you, too. Seems we have a lot in common."

Alex squirmed in his seat. "Yeah?"

Kenji winked. "We're both nervous about seeing our children for the first time today."

"Huh. That's true. You're nervous?"

"Of course. She has every right to hate me. Maybe you could put in a good word for me?"

"I'm right here," Zoey said.

Kenji didn't take his eyes off Alex. "She has her mom's spunk. Have you ever noticed that?"

A slow smile spread across Alex's face. "Yeah, that's true."

Zoey glared at Alex. Whose side was he on, anyway?

Valerie started the car. "At least someone's being respectful to you." She gave Zoey a disapproving look to which Zoey promptly returned one of her own. "Are we ready?"

Zoey's mouth went dry. What was going on? How could she be in the car with her dad on the way to find out if her child was a boy or a girl? She took Alex's hand and gave it a squeeze. He lifted her hand and gave it a light kiss. Then he gave her a look that told her everything would be okay.

Temptation

C HAD WAS TOO frustrated to go back home and face Alex and Zoey. Why couldn't the cops get answers? Either the body was Macy's or it wasn't. Was it really that difficult with all the technology available?

If they would have at least let him look at the body, he could have told them whether or not it was her. If he wasn't so sure, he wouldn't be arguing with Alyssa.

As much as he loved her, he wasn't going to give in and say he thought Macy was gone. He didn't believe it and he wasn't going to let anyone think he did. When she returned home, he wanted to be able to look her in the eyes and tell her he hadn't given up on her, not for a moment.

She was going to return. Each passing day only brought Macy's return closer. He was sure of it. He wasn't going to judge Alyssa for her stance, but he wasn't going to take it with her. Even if it meant damaging their marriage. She was the one who wouldn't agree to disagree. They could still live under the same roof and hold different beliefs.

The car was suffocating. He pulled into the parking lot of the closest park. He would walk around the trails to burn off some energy. He couldn't think straight. Between the cops and Alyssa, he'd had about all he could take.

That wasn't true. The lack of results and Alyssa's demands were the icing on the cake of his life. He'd already had all he could take between his two kids. Anyone else in his shoes would have lost their minds already. He was actually holding everything together pretty well.

He slammed his door shut and locked it with the remote. Aside from a few random joggers, the park was empty. He looked up at the sky with the menacing clouds. No wonder only the die hards were out. Chad didn't care if he ended up soaked. He had energy to burn. Even though he wasn't dressed for a run, he was taking one.

Lifting weights had been one way he used to clear his head, but he hadn't even looked at those in months. He broke into a run and passed everyone else jogging. His lungs burned, but he didn't care. It actually felt good.

By the time the trail circled around and he was back where he started, he was almost completely out of breath. He had given himself fully to the run. He hadn't paid any attention to the scenery around him or given himself the chance to think about anything. None of his problems crossed his mind as he ran through the length of the trail.

He stopped at a bench, leaning his arm against the back of it, gasping for air. Sweat ran down his face, neck and back. He wiped it out of his eyes, wishing he had thought to bring something to drink. His mouth was parched.

Chad was vaguely aware of footsteps behind him, but he didn't really care.

"Hey, Chad, I thought that was you. What are you doing running in slacks?"

He turned around to face Lydia. "Do you follow me everywhere I go?" he asked in between gasps for air.

"Maybe. What are you doing out here?"

"I needed some exercise."

"In those shoes?"

"What's wrong with my shoes?"

"They're not exactly running shoes. You're going to have some painful blisters."

"I don't really care." He sat down on the other side of the bench.

"Well, you should. If you're going take care of—"

"Don't lecture me."

Lydia sat next to Chad. "I'm not lecturing. I'm concerned. I know we're done, but I still love you."

"Don't say that."

"Chad, it's true."

He stared her in the eyes. "That doesn't mean you need to tell me."

"I can't just walk away when you're clearly in some kind of trouble."

"I'm not in trouble. I just needed some air." He looked away. The clouds were getting darker, just like his mood.

A hand rested on his shoulder. "Is it Macy?"

Chad pushed her hand away. "Damn it, Lydia. Would you keep your hands off?"

She looked hurt. "Where's Alyssa?"

He stood up. "Would you just leave me alone? I didn't ask you to come and check on me. Go away."

"If that's what you really want. Is it?"

"What I want is for everything to return to the way it was before my daughter went missing."

"That's when we were together."

"Before that. It was a mistake. I should have worked on my marriage instead of turning to you."

"I'm not trying to pull you away from your family, Chad. You looked distressed and because I care, I had to check on you. I don't want to leave you like this because it's obvious that something's going on. If you want to talk about something, tell me. No one else is around and I'm not going to tell anyone anything. You know that much. Your secrets are safe with me."

He stared into her dark eyes. She looked like she meant it, and he did know she could keep a secret. Lydia also had a way of making him feel better when the world seemed against him.

It was dangerous territory, but who else did he have to talk with? Most of his friends had stopped contacting him because no one knew what to say about Macy's disappearance. It wasn't like they were the kind of buddies he could pour his heart out to anyway. Over the last few years, he had pushed everyone away while he worked on the blog. He was a big man on the Internet, but what had it gotten him?

"My life is falling apart on every front."

"I'm listening."

"You swear to keep this to yourself?"

"Your secrets are always safe with me," Lydia repeated.

Chad paused, running his hands through his hair. He looked around to make sure no one else was close enough to hear. "Alex…he got a girl pregnant."

Lydia's eyes widened. "I'm so sorry."

"He's only thirteen and she's going through with everything. They might give it up for adoption, but they're not going to decide anything yet. I'm sure this is all because of Macy being gone, but it makes her disappearance that much harder to deal with."

"How's Alex handling it?"

Chad shook his head. "I don't think he understands the gravity of the situation. He keeps pushing me away, though, so I don't know. I can't figure out what he's thinking."

"Like you said, he's only thirteen. It's a difficult age. He's trying to figure out who he is."

"That's exactly why he doesn't need to be a dad! He's not even close to ready, no matter what he thinks." Tears filled his eyes and he brushed them away.

"Oh, Chad. Is there anything I can do? Do you guys need anything?"

"No. We just have to take it one day at a time. All I can do is hope that the kids make the right decision. I'm not raising it for them."

"What does Alyssa think?"

"She's not happy, but that's the least of our problems."

Lydia raised an eyebrow, but said nothing.

Chad wiped at new tears. "She's staying with a friend. Lyss thinks Macy is dead, and she's mad I don't." He broke down and cried into his hands. "What if she doesn't come back home?" He leaned forward, resting his elbows on his lap as he let out gut-wrenching sobs. His body shook, and he thought he felt Lydia wrap an arm around him, but he wasn't sure and didn't care enough to fight her.

His life was falling apart and there was nothing he could do about it. He couldn't hold it together anymore—that much was clear. Why else would he be crying in the middle of a park? He wiped his nose with his sleeve and seeing the disgusting mess, he hid it before Lydia could see it.

She pulled her purse into her lap and then handed him a small pack of tissues.

Chad took it and wiped his face and then tried to be discreet wiping his sleeve. He took another one and put it to his face, feeling another round of sobs coming. His chest tightened, and the lump in his throat felt like it was going to explode. He shook harder than before, foreign sounds escaping his throat as his crying intensified.

Lydia rubbed his back, telling him that it was okay to let it out.

He cried all the more. Chad thought about his wife and both of their kids—and the gigantic mess they all had. What had happened to the days when he had been able to fix most problems with a kiss? Kissing scrapes and bruises for the kids and some romance for Alyssa. None of that worked anymore. He was helpless to fix any of their problems or hurts. He couldn't even help himself. And now he was sobbing in public, being comforted by his former lover.

This was rock bottom. Things couldn't get any worse than this. No, that wasn't true. The DNA results could come in and prove that he would never get to see his daughter again. That would be rock bottom.

He continued to sob until there was nothing left. Not another tear would come. Chad pulled more tissues from the little pack and wiped his face and blew his nose several times. He looked over at Lydia and noticed it was raining.

Lightning flashed in the distance. "Should we get inside?"

"We don't have to. It's pretty far away."

"But it's raining."

Lydia shrugged. "It's up to you."

"I don't care about getting soaked. You probably do."

She shook her head. "I'm more worried about you. Are you going to be okay?"

Chad looked into her eyes. Her hair was soaked, dripping onto her coat. She looked beautiful, especially with the look on her face mixed with concern and love. It was nice to have someone who cared about him. Someone who wanted to be there for him without needing anything.

Lydia stared back into his eyes, not saying anything or moving. Her expression showed how much she cared about him.

Chad knew she didn't judge him for believing his daughter was alive. He moved his face closer to hers. He wanted to kiss her and forget about everything else in the world. She could make him forget his troubles, even if it was only for a short time. The world could be right again.

Eagerness filled her eyes as Chad moved at a snail's pace closer to her. He just wanted to make all of his problems disappear and she could do that for him. And she would too.

Chad stopped and pulled back, shaking his head. "I can't. I can't do this."

"You don't have to. I'm here for you, however you need me."

Regret washed over him. He wasn't even sure what for. Because of the mistakes he had made? For pushing his family away? For loving Lydia? For wanting her at that moment while his daughter was in trouble?

More tears filled his eyes and he broke into another crying fit. How much of this did he have in him? Chad had held himself together for so long and now everything was unraveling. As his tears fell, the rain drops landed on his shirt, soaking into his back. He didn't care. He could get pneumonia and die for all he cared. Everyone else would be better off with him gone anyway.

He looked up at Lydia. She had tears shining in her eyes.

"What's wrong?"

"I hate seeing you like this. It's killing me that you hurt so much."

Chad put his face back into his hands, allowing the sobs to take over. Why was it that Lydia cared so much about him and Alyssa seemed to despise him again? And for what? Because he wouldn't say Macy could have a funeral? He wasn't going to give his child a funeral unless she was dead, and he had no reason to believe that she was.

He shook, feeling as though he would collapse soon. At least he was with someone who actually cared about him, even if he couldn't allow himself to give into his own feelings for her. Despite the fact that Alyssa was staying with Sharon instead of him, he was going to remain faithful to her. It wasn't like she was staying with another man.

Hiding

MACY ROLLED OVER, bumping into something. She rubbed her eyes, trying to remember where she was. A blank wall faced her and she was squished. She looked over to see Heather sleeping next to her. Everything from the previous day came rushing back.

What were they going to do? After she had told Heather everything, they were both exhausted and decided to share the small bed.

The lock on the outside of the door made a jiggling noise. Heather sat up and stared at Macy. She jumped out of bed and ran to the far corner of the room.

Candice came in and looked at Macy. "I talked the other nurses into letting you sleep in today. How do you feel?"

Macy stretched. "I haven't slept that well in a long time." Candice had no idea just how true that was.

"I'm glad to hear it. My shift is over and I'll be off a few days. Please be good. We really just want you to get out of here. I want nothing more than to see you back on the street, hanging out with your friends. You've been here entirely too long. You should have just been here for a day or two of observation. Can you play nice for a couple days?"

Macy nodded.

"I'm serious, Heather. You need to get back to school and see your friends again. You were such a good girl before your mom took off. I wish she would come back and take responsibility. She has no idea what she's doing to you."

Macy looked over at Heather from the corner of her eyes. She looked furious. Macy looked back to Candice. "I'll do my best."

She didn't look convinced. "Just go along with the program, and you'll be out before you know it. Even if you don't like it, accept reality. That will be your first step toward healing and getting out of here."

"Okay," said Macy.

Candice raised an eyebrow. "Really? You're not going to fight me and try to convince me that your mom isn't in Paris?"

Macy shook her head. "First step toward healing. I have to accept the facts."

"Wow. I'm impressed, Heather. Maybe you actually will be out in time to enjoy your summer. Keep it up." She disappeared and closed the door. Macy could hear it lock.

Heather moved to the bed, still looking angry. "How could you agree with her like that? I thought you were on my side and believe my mom's dead."

"I am and I do, but it's not going to do either of us any good if we keep trying to convince them. They're not going to do anything about it, anyway. We need to get out of here, and then we'll go to the police. I think they have to listen. Let's just focus on one thing at a time. First, getting out of here. Next, getting your dad in jail for a long, long time. Hopefully a life sentence."

Heather took a deep breath and nodded. "It's a good thing she talked with you, because I can't put up a front like that. No way am I going to let anyone get away with saying that Mom is a home-wrecker. Not when she was a loving mom. Why won't anyone listen to me?"

Macy slid her feet to the ground. "Because your dad is the one convincing them otherwise. What he wants, he gets. But that's about to end."

The door opened again and Heather darted back to the corner. A new nurse looked at Macy. "Is it true? I hear that you might have a change of heart?"

"Maybe," said Macy.

"Let's see how well you handle time with some others. Can you be nice if we let you spend some time with other kids?"

Macy looked over at Heather, not sure what to do. Heather nodded and indicated for her to go with her.

"Of course I can," Macy said. She gave a convincing look.

"We can't risk another incident like last time. If you show even a sign of doing that again, I'll have no other choice except to bring you right back here. Or worse."

Macy looked back at Heather. She shrugged her shoulders and had a slight smile on her face.

"I won't act up."

"Glad to hear it. Come on."

Macy went with the nurse, not sure what to expect. Heather had dark circles under her eyes, so maybe she would get some more sleep. Macy had a feeling that she had gotten less sleep than Macy over the months. Hopefully, she would just sleep and not do anything to jeopardize them getting out.

The nurse led her to a small cafeteria. "There's a guard posted by the door. He knows to keep an eye on you. Got it?"

"Sure."

"Have a seat and someone will bring you a tray. Remember, the better behaved you are, the more likely you will be to get out of here."

"I know. I'm ready for change." Macy made her way to one of the tables. She sat away from the others. It was nice to be around kids again, but she didn't want to get close to anyone. What if someone figured out that she wasn't Heather?

Some of the kids whispered, but no one actually paid her any attention. At least she was used to being treated much worse at school. Being ignored was nice compared to being mooed at, like at her school cafeteria. That was why she had started eating lunch in the bathroom and then gave up lunch altogether. Even after she lost all that weight, the kids at school only saw Muffin Top Macy.

Her blood pressure went up and took some deep breaths. This wasn't the time to think about it. Heather's anger is what had kept her there for so long. In order for the both of them to get out, she needed to keep her cool.

Without a word, someone came in and set a tray of food in front of her. Although she was glad to not have to cook, the food didn't look at all appealing. Stiff-looking spaghetti sat on the middle of the plate with ground meat sauce sliding down. Applesauce was slopped next to it, reminding her of the pigs' feed at the farm. Burnt green beans were off to the side.

Regardless of how it looked, she needed to eat. She picked up the fork and started with the applesauce, because it looked the least offensive. It tasted okay, though it was a little dry. She could feel eyes on her as she ate.

Macy pictured her family. Getting back to them was the goal. She needed to act sweet and happy regardless of how anyone treated her. These people didn't matter, but getting back home did. What if she could be back that day? Her heart sped up.

She thought about Alex running around the bonus room, singing to his favorite songs. He loved creating his own "music videos," and she was usually the one who held his phone to record it. What she wouldn't give to do that again. She had complained countless times about it before, but now she'd gladly record him for hours.

Despite the level of nastiness of the food, she felt better. She'd had a decent night's sleep and now a meal. Macy was ready to get home. She looked around, not sure what to do. The room had emptied somewhat, leaving only a few more kids.

One of them got up and put his tray on a counter and left the room. Macy did the same and followed the sounds of conversation. She found herself in a large room full of kids. Some were watching TV, others were playing games or writing, and another girl sat by a window reading.

Macy walked in, nerves on edge. No one seemed to notice her. She sat down on a couch and watched everyone. Her eyes were drawn to the movie. It was a PG one she had seen when she was a kid, but it had been so long since she had watched TV, she wanted to watch anyway. She didn't have the best angle, but she didn't want to join the others. If Heather had freaked out on them, who knew how they would react to her?

When the movie ended, the nurse who had given Macy her food turned the TV off. The other kids watching groaned and complained before dispersing around the room.

The nurse came over to Macy. "How are you doing? I haven't heard a single complaint about you. That's really good news."

"Like I told the other nurse, I'm ready to go home. I'll do whatever it takes to get there."

"Given your history, it's going to take some time, but if you keep this up, you'll find yourself on the outside soon. Despite what you believe, we're all on your side. We want to see you go back home and to school where you belong."

Macy nodded. She felt bad for Heather. No one would listen to her about her mom—thanks to Chester—and it hadn't gone well. She was desperate for someone to believe her. Macy could understand that. She'd been desperate to get out of the community, and look what had happened. Tears stung her eyes. She was going to have to live with that guilt the rest of her life.

"Tears?" asked the nurse. "You must be telling the truth. I'm glad to see you letting your guard down, Heather. Do you think you're ready to talk with the doctor again? This time without throwing things around his office."

"Yeah." Her voice cracked. She suddenly felt overwhelmed. The tears spilled onto her face.

The nurse sat next to her. "Is there anything you want to talk about?"

"It's all my fault."

"What is?"

"Everything." She pulled her feet onto the couch and then rested her face on her knees. She cried, not caring how loud she was or who was looking. She continued to cry until she had nothing left. When she looked up, the nurse still watched her. She handed Macy a tissue and then asked, "Do you feel better?"

She didn't, but Macy nodded, not finding any words. She just wanted to go back home.

"I think the doctor would clear his schedule if you're ready to talk with him."

Macy wiped her face. "I am. Can we stop off at my room first?"

"What for?"

"Please."

"Sure. Let's go." She led Macy back to Heather's room. Macy looked around for Heather and found her hiding near the door again. She motioned for Heather to come out.

Heather looked at her like she was crazy. Macy motioned some more until Heather came out and stood next to her.

The nurse looked back and forth between Heather and Macy, wide eyed. "What...? How did...? What's going on?"

Macy looked her in the eyes. "The two of us, we want to speak to the doctor. We need to be heard."

Results

CHAD KICKED OFF his wet shoes and closed the door behind him. His clothes clung to him and he needed to get those off as well. Even though he was inside, rain water ran down from his hair into his face. He wiped it away.

"Is anyone home?"

The house was unusually quiet. Had Alex gone to Zoey's appointment already?

"Alex, are you here?"

Silence. He shivered as water slid down his back. He would have to dry out the inside of his car as well, but first he needed to get a shower. He felt empty inside after having sobbed and poured his heart out to Lydia.

He had been afraid she was going to take his outpouring of grief the wrong way, but she kept her word and acted like a friend. She had listened and consoled, not giving him a judging word or look once. His heart ached. Why wouldn't Alyssa treat him like that? Who was he kidding? He knew the answer to that. She was stuck in her own heartache.

Neither one of them was able to give what the other needed. Maybe this time apart *was* what they needed. Hopefully Sharon, or whoever she was staying with, was able to give her the same kind of friendship that Lydia had given him.

"Is anyone home? Final chance to speak up before I strip."

No one responded, so Chad pulled his shirt off, though it clung to him, fighting to stay on. He threw it on the tiled floor and then attempted to pull his pants off too. The drenched jeans fought even more than the shirt had. He had to sit on the stairs and play tug-of-war with them to finally get them off.

He grabbed the shirt and then threw the clothes in the laundry room on the way to his bedroom. He took a shower and put on dry clothes, and then he noticed his cell phone sitting on the bed. The light was blinking, so he picked it up to see what he had missed. Maybe it was Alyssa wanting to talk. His heart tightened at the hope of working things out with her.

Chad scrolled to the notifications and saw that he did have a missed call, but it wasn't from his wife. It was from Detective Fleshman. His heart exploded into a fit of beats. He couldn't explain it, but he could feel deep down that whatever Fleshman had to say was going to be a game changer.

There were no messages, so he called the detective back.

"Chad?"

"What's going on? I left my phone at home, so I missed your call."

"There's been a break in the case. Are you sitting down?"

The room shrunk around him. He sat on the bed, preparing for the worst. "I am now."

"We finally got the results."

Chad held his breath. "And?"

"It's not her. The DNA proves that the body isn't your daughter. The girl we found had connections to a cult commune we've been trying to find."

Chad fell back on the bed, having only heard that the body wasn't Macy. "I knew it wasn't her." Tears of gratitude filled his eyes. "What now?"

"Prepare for another media frenzy."

"Of course. But what about the case? What about Macy? We need to find her. Everything has been focused on that body for too long. She's out there somewhere—and she's alive. We have to find her."

"It's time to go through all of the clues with a fine tooth comb. We need to re-investigate clues that didn't get enough attention before. Word needs to get out again for people to keep an eye out for her. I've got someone working on doctoring her photos again to show what she would look like with different haircuts and colors."

"Thank you." Chad couldn't find the words to express his gratitude.

His chest tightened, making it difficult to breathe.

Fleshman continued talking, now about the cult again, but Chad couldn't focus. Something about the mountains.

Chad interrupted him mid-sentence. "Can I call you back?"

"Of course. You've got my number."

"Thanks." Chad ended the call and pushed his phone away. He gave into another fit of sobs. He shook, cried, wailed, and even yelled. When he calmed down, he started to drift off to sleep when he heard something in the hall. "Is someone there?" He allowed himself the hope that it was actually Macy, not that she would be able to get in with the new locks and security codes.

"It's me." Alyssa appeared in the doorway.

Chad sat up, rubbing dried tears. His eyes felt puffy.

"Are you all right?" She looked concerned.

"Yeah. I just got off the phone with Fleshman."

She nodded. "I talked with him a little while ago."

"Is that why you're here?"

Alyssa nodded. She sat down next to him, looking deep in thought.

"Are you coming back home?" he asked.

Alyssa looked into his eyes and her face softened. "It kills me to see you so upset. Look at you." She ran the backs of her fingers along his face. "You're a mess."

"Our baby is alive. We have the proof now."

She stared at him, not saying anything.

"Don't you believe it now?"

Her fingers went down and traced his back. "We know that one girl isn't her."

"Macy's alive. She's coming back to us. Why can't you believe that?"

Tears shone in her eyes. "It's been so long, Chad. You know that. We've suffered through this for what feels like an eternity. April is almost here. Where would she be?"

"I don't know that I want to know, but one day she's going to tell us herself."

She rubbed his arm, staring into his eyes.

He cupped her chin in his palm. "Please come back home, Lyss. I can't lose you, too."

Alyssa's lips shook and tears spilled onto her cheeks. She nodded. "We'll see how it goes. You know, agreeing to disagree. If you're right, and I really wish you were, we'll see what happens with the new media campaign. Maybe something will come up proving me wrong. I've never hoped to be wrong more in my life."

"You still don't believe she's coming home." It wasn't a question— and it ripped his heart into pieces.

"I want to, but I can't lie."

They continued staring into each other's eyes. There was so much he wanted to say, but he was afraid of sending her running again. "I've missed you. Please stay home. I need you."

Something in her face changed. Her entire face twisted, and she leaned into his chest and sobbed. He wrapped his arms around her, pulling her close. She cried for a while and soon Chad found himself back in tears. He had never cried so much in his life, but it felt good.

He wasn't sure how much time passed; it seemed to stop completely except that the sky cleared and the room lit up.

Alyssa sat back. "I have something to confess."

Chad's heart skipped a beat. "What?"

She looked pained. "I…how do I say this?"

"Just tell me."

"I got the impression you think I've been staying with Sharon, but I haven't."

He couldn't speak. What did she mean? Where was she going with this? Chad knew if she was about to say she had been staying with some guy—who he would kill—he really had no room to judge. He couldn't blame her, not after his relationship with Lydia. But the other man, sure, he could murder him. There wasn't a jury around that would blame him.

Alyssa took a deep breath. "I've been staying with a guy named Rusty."

"Who the hell is Rusty?"

Her eyes widened, begging him to hear her out. "I've been staying in his guest room—alone. He lost his family, his entire family. That's how we started talking in the first place. But nothing happened. I swear."

"What do you mean nothing happened? You've been staying with some guy? Some random stranger? You can't tell me nothing happened." He knew he was being a hypocrite, but he didn't care. Anger burned within him at the thought of her being with another man.

She explained going to the bar and how he had told the waitress to stop bringing drinks and then refused to let her drive home.

"He could have towed you here. You realize that, don't you?"

"I know." She paused. "He did, the first time."

"What first time?"

"It was shortly after Macy disappeared. I couldn't take it and one night, I snuck out and ended up at the bar. I could barely speak, and he got me back home safely."

"When was that? I don't remember you going anywhere."

She frowned. "You slept through the whole thing."

Chad shook his head, the weight of what he had done with Lydia sinking in. If he felt this horrible just hearing about Alyssa staying at the house of some guy, how much worse would she feel knowing he'd had a relationship with Lydia before Macy disappeared?

"I swear, Chad, nothing happened. If you met him, you'd know right away that he's not over the loss of his family. Their pictures and their stuff is all over the house. It's like they just stepped out to go shopping or something."

"Why go to his house?"

"I was going to sleep in my car since I couldn't drive. He wanted to tow me home, but I needed space to think—and sleep apparently. I've never slept so much as I have the last few days. But anyway, since I wouldn't go home, he offered his guest room. I poured my heart out, and he listened. That's about it. If it makes you feel any better, it helped me to realize how much I wanted to get back and pour my heart out to you instead."

Chad nodded. "I had a similar experience."

Her eyes widened. "You did?"

"This morning I'd had all I could take. I ended up at a park, running around the trail." He pulled his feet up and rubbed his blisters. "I ran into Lydia Harris from the HOA and ended up sobbing in the park."

"Lydia? Isn't her husband always out of town?"

"Yeah."

"Don't get too close to her. She's lonely. I can see it in her eyes."

"I won't." Guilt stung at him for not telling Alyssa the entire story, but she didn't need to know everything. It was over. He wasn't going to see her, or anyone else for that matter, again. He was one hundred percent devoted to Alyssa as long as she would have him. If she knew about Lydia, it would crush her. He couldn't do that to her after everything that had already happened with Macy and Alex.

It would definitely be the end of their relationship—and he couldn't handle that. He regretted ever talking to Lydia with everything in him. He would never make that mistake again. He belonged to Alyssa wholly. They needed each other now more than ever. His guilt was punishment enough. There was no reason to break her heart. She didn't deserve it.

She ran her hand along his arm, giving him the chills. "We'll pour our souls out to each other only from now on. Right?"

"You've got it."

Alyssa leaned over and placed her soft lips on his. He pulled her closer, kissing her back.

Both of their phones rang.

They pulled back, giving each other confused looks.

Chad looked at his. "It's Fleshman."

"Reynolds. Something is going on." She slid her finger across the screen.

Chad did the same on his. "Fleshman? What's going on?"

Next to him, Alyssa talked to Reynolds, and he couldn't understand what either Fleshman or Alyssa were saying.

"Hold on, Detective." Chad went out into the hall. "I couldn't hear you. What were you saying?"

"We might not have to wait on the media. We already have a break in the case."

"Another one?"

"There's a girl several hours away claiming to be your daughter. There's a catch though."

The hall spun around Chad. He leaned against the wall. "What?"

"She's in a mental hospital, but the nurses are freaked out because they thought she was someone else. I'm more than a little confused, but we need to get over there and figure this out. They're not releasing her until they have proof that she is who she says."

His throat closed up.

"Chad? Are you still there?"

Somehow he managed to find his voice. "Text me the address. We'll be right there."

"Try not to get your hopes up. We—"

"Just text me the address." Chad ended the call. Could this really be it? Was he about to see Macy again? Or would this be yet another heartache?

He looked into the bedroom. Alyssa was on the phone with tears running down her face. He wanted to comfort her, but he needed to call Alex first. He would want to join them. He needed to know too.

Alex answered right away. "Dad, can you call me back later? We're about to find out if it's a boy or a girl. It took forever to get in."

"Okay. Your mom and I are going with the detective for a while. There have been some developments in the case. Check the news when you can."

"Wait. What?"

"The body isn't Macy, son. It looks like she's alive."

"She's alive?"

Chad could hear exclamations from Zoey and Valerie on the other end. "I'll call you in a few hours and we can exchange news."

Breakdown

WHEN THEY PULLED into the parking lot of the Shady Hills Mental Health Facility, Alyssa saw Detective Fleshman and Officer Anderson getting out of their police cruiser.

She didn't wait for Chad to fully stop the car before she jumped out and ran to the police.

"What's going on? Where's my baby?"

"That's what we need to figure out," Anderson said, tipping his hat. "There's a girl named Heather claiming to be Macy. She's been in there longer that Macy's been missing, so we—"

"No, there's two girls they thought were Heather," Fleshman corrected.

"And the strange thing is that when the Mercers' house was broken into, the intruder mentioned someone named Heather. Do you remember that?" He flipped through his notepad. "See? Right here. Zoey said he called Macy's room Heather's."

Alyssa looked at them like they had lost their minds. "What?"

Fleshman gave her an apologetic look. "It's complicated. We'll wait for Chad and then get in there and figure out what's going on."

Chad ran up to them. "Is Macy in there?" He looked as desperate as Alyssa felt. He took Alyssa's hand.

"That's what we're here to find out," said Anderson.

"Would you just take us to our daughter?" Alyssa blurted out. "I'm sorry. I can't go another minute without seeing her."

"Sorry. Let's go."

Fleshman walked toward the building and Alyssa hurried to keep up. Her heart raced. Would this be the end of the nightmare or merely another dead end? She prayed Macy would be inside.

When they got inside, Anderson explained what was going on to the lady at the front desk. Alyssa had to bite her tongue. She wanted to scream for her to let them in.

The receptionist looked through some notes. "I see that they're expecting you. Have a seat and someone will come for you soon."

Alyssa squeezed Chad's hand. She looked at the big doors they would go through. She would rip them off their hinges if she had to. She would give them one minute to send someone before she started making demands.

Fleshman and Anderson both took seats, but Chad and Alyssa remained standing. Alyssa kept her attention on the big clock on the wall. As soon as one minute passed, she looked at Fleshman. "What's taking them so long?"

"Give them some time. This building is enormous. Even if they come for us right away, it could be five or ten minutes."

"Five or ten minutes? I can't wait that long."

The officers exchanged a look and then Anderson turned to Alyssa. "You've been patient all this time. Give it a few more minutes and then you might get to see your daughter. We don't know, but we really need you to remain calm. Can you do that?"

Chad squeezed her hand. "We will. You won't regret allowing us to come along with you."

Fleshman nodded. "Good to hear. We don't know that we'll see her right away. Maybe we will, maybe we won't. Just follow our lead and hopefully you'll have your daughter in your arms soon enough."

"They'll let her out, right?" Alyssa asked. "Why is she even in here?"

Anderson shook his head. "We don't have those answers yet."

"What answers *do* you have?"

"Not a lot," Fleshman said. "There's a girl here who's been giving the staff trouble since before Macy disappeared. Her parents are out of the picture and—"

"What does this have to do with my child?" Alyssa demanded.

Chad gave her hand a gentle squeeze. "Lyss, let him talk."

"I don't see how you can stay so calm."

"Because I don't want to be sent outside while they go in and see Macy."

Alyssa looked back to Fleshman, clenching her fists. "Continue."

"This other girl, Heather, she's been claiming that her dad killed her mom. She's in denial that her mom left them. The staff says it's a real sad case, but earlier today, there were two of her. Another girl appeared somehow, who looks just like her. The only way they can tell the difference is that the new one has shorter hair, but it's the same length as Heather's when she came in months ago."

"What's your point?" Alyssa asked.

"The second one is claiming that she's Macy. She says she was kidnapped by Heather's dad and she also believes that he killed Heather's mom."

Alyssa leaned against Chad. "I…I don't understand."

Chad held her tight. "You mean that the other dad, he took Macy to replace his daughter?"

"It's beginning to look that way," Anderson said. "The local authorities are said to be questioning him now. There are a lot of pieces to be put together. A big one is you two identifying whether or not the second girl is in fact Macy."

"Do you have a picture?" Alyssa asked. "Why won't they let us in there? What's taking them so long?" She pulled away from Chad and ran to the front desk, her vision more blurry by the moment. Blinking the tears onto her face, she stared down the receptionist. "Let us in there! My daughter has been missing since November! I *need* to see her."

"I'm sorry. We have strict protocol. You must have a staff member escort you in."

"You're staff!" Alyssa slammed her hand on the desk, causing the receptionist to jump. She looked at her name tag. "Look, Lynette. I don't know if you have children, but not knowing where your child is, that's the worst feeling in the world. It gets even harder the more time passes. When they're little and run out of your sight at the mall for a minute, sheer terror runs through you. Ever been there? If they hide somewhere, making that terror go for another five minutes, that's hell. I've been there once when my son was little. Can you imagine those five minutes turning into almost half a year? There isn't a word to describe that!"

Lynette was visibly shaken. "I—I'm really sorry for everything you've been through. I don't have kids, but my niece, one time she ran off when I was taking care of her. I kind of understand what you're saying. I wish I could do something for you."

"Let me in! Take me to my daughter...please." More tears fell to her cheeks.

Alyssa felt hands on her shoulders. "Let's go wait with the officers, Lyss."

"Take me in there," Alyssa begged.

Lynette shook. "I'm really sorry. I don't have the key card to get in."

"Damn you people!" Alyssa shook her shoulder to get past Chad and ran to the big, metal door. She banged on it. "I'm coming, baby! I'll be there as soon as I can." Her fists hurt as she pounded, but she didn't care.

Hands pulled her away. They dragged her back to the waiting area. "Stop! I need to get to Macy." She pushed against Chad, who held her even tighter. "Let go of me."

Fleshman appeared in front of her. "Mrs. Mercer, you need to get control of yourself now. Do you understand me? We brought you with us because we thought you would be able to help us. If you keep acting like this, we're going to have no choice except to take you into custody."

She stopped struggling. "You would arrest me?"

"That's the last thing I want to do after everything you've been through. Your daughter may very well be on the other side of those doors, but we need your cooperation. It will be a lot easier if you stay calm. The big question is: do you want to be with your husband when he identifies the girl as either your daughter or not?"

"Of course I do."

"It won't be much longer. You've waited this long. Can you wait another few minutes until someone comes for us?"

"Fine." Alyssa pushed against Chad, who let go of her. She sat down on a chair near the window and stared out. How dare they think they could arrest her? After everything she'd been through? The two of them, they *knew*. They had been working closely with her and Chad. They had been in daily contact for a while.

Chad sat on the floor in front of her, resting his hands on her knees. "I know how you feel, Lyss. Really, I do. I want to scream and break things, but it won't do any good. For the first time since she disappeared, we have real hope—real reason to believe that she's alive and safe. It's killing me that she could be in this very building, but we still can't get to her."

"This is worse than torture. They have no clue what this is like."

He shook his head. "We're so close, yet so far. But we have to hold it together—for Macy. She's been through more than we can imagine. If what Fleshman said is true, she been with a kidnapper all this time. Not only that, but she's going to get home and find out that she's going to be an aunt. We're going to have to hold it together, no matter how much we feel like falling apart."

"I've been doing nothing other than holding myself together for all these long, terrifying months."

"But this time, we'll have Macy with us. I hope to God that's the case, anyway."

She nodded. "I'll be strong for her. That's what I've been doing all along."

Chad grabbed her hands and slid his fingers between hers. They sat in silence for what felt like an eternity. Alyssa looked out the window for a little while, and then she looked back to Chad, who had his chin rested on her lap. Tears shone in his eyes and the pained expression on his face broke her already-crushed heart.

"Oh, Chad."

He looked up at her and the tears spilled to his cheeks. She let go of his hand and wiped the tears away. He sat up and stared into her eyes, more tears falling. She leaned forward and kissed his tears. He put his hands on her face and kissed her lips.

Chad pulled back and stared at her. "Are we going to be okay, Lyss? Will you come back home to me?"

"Yes."

"Would you even if Macy wasn't coming home?"

Alyssa paused. The pain on his face made her heart hurt. "I wouldn't go anywhere else. I need you."

He pulled her into another kiss. "And I need you. I've never been surer of that than at this moment."

Someone cleared their throat behind them. "They're ready for us."

Alyssa turned around to see Detective Fleshman and Officer Anderson standing with a man in a white lab coat. She stood, but her legs wouldn't support her weight. She fell toward the ground, but Chad caught her.

"Lean against me."

She put all her weight against him. He kept his arms around her and somehow she managed to walk. "Are we really about to see Macy?" Alyssa whispered.

"I hope so." Though he held her with strong arms, Alyssa could feel him shaking. He was just as scared as she was.

Alyssa didn't know what scared her more, finding out that the girl wasn't Macy or hearing about what her daughter had gone through all the time she was missing. Had she been abused? They said the abductor had been trying to replace his daughter. Was there a chance that he had treated her well?

The large, metal door opened slowly. Alyssa's heart sank as she saw another heavy door. How long would it take to get to Macy? What would she do if the girl wasn't Macy? What would she if the girl *was*?

Doors

C HAD'S THROAT CLOSED up as the final metal door shut behind them. He looked at the scene in front of him. It looked like a typical hospital with another reception area and doors with numbers.

The doctor—what had he said his name was?—stopped and said something to the receptionist. He turned back to them. "I sure hope you will be able to offer some insight. We're still trying to figure out how this happened. Sure, we get kids trying to sneak out, but never in. This is a first."

"Where is she?" Alyssa asked, her voice strained.

Chad gave her shoulders a squeeze.

"They're in Heather's room and they're both sticking to the same story since we discovered the two of them."

"Lead the way," Fleshman said.

Chad looked at the doctor's tag. Dr. Jones, that was right. He focused on the door numbers as they walked down the hall. He couldn't bear to think about seeing Macy, or worse, not seeing her. What if neither of those girls were her? Could this be the practical joke of a sick girl who belonged in a mental hospital?

Dr. Jones stopped in front of a door and used a key to open the door.

Chad held his breath and exchanged and worried, nervous look with Alyssa. Her skin looked pale. He was sure his was too. Were they about to finally see Macy?

The doctor held the door open and motioned for them to come in.

Chad took Alyssa's hand and walked in with her. His heart pounded and felt as though it would jump out of his throat. He looked around the room, and his gaze settled on two girls. They looked exactly the same, and neither had Macy's dark hair, but they both had her beautiful face. He looked back and forth between them.

The one on the right smiled. "Mom! Dad!" She ran into both of them, wrapping one arm around Chad and the other around Alyssa. She squeezed hard and then started sobbing.

Chad was in shock and had to force himself to wrap his free arm around her. It was her, it was actually her. He had hugged her so many times, he would know her anywhere. He held her tighter, vaguely aware of Alyssa's sobs over Macy's. She kept saying Macy's name over and over again.

It didn't feel real. He had believed she was alive somewhere, but now that she was there in his arms, he wasn't sure what was going on. It was like he was afraid to believe it was real.

He rested his face on top of her head. "Is it really you, Macy?" he whispered.

"Daddy, I'm so sorry for everything. I'll never sneak out again. I swear."

Tears filled his eyes and soaked her hair. "And there's so much I'm going to do differently, baby. So much. I'm sorry for not listening to you and not...." Chad couldn't find his voice. He kissed the top of her head.

"I hate to break up this reunion, but we need to discuss some matters."

Chad looked up at the officers and the doctor. "As long as we get to take her home, we can talk about whatever you want."

Dr. Jones nodded. "Let's take this to my office. There's room for everyone to sit."

They followed the doctor, neither Chad nor Alyssa letting go of Macy. He watched Alyssa stroke Macy's hair the whole way to the office. The three of them sat on a couch with Macy in the middle. She kept looking back and forth between them.

"Are you okay?" Chad asked. "What have you been through?"

"All I wanted was to get back to you guys." She pushed her face into Chad's chest. "I'm so sorry for everything."

Fresh tears filled Chad's eyes. "You have nothing to be sorry about." He wrapped his arms around her, never wanting to let go. Alyssa leaned her head against Macy's, and Chad wrapped an arm around her too.

They sat like that for a minute, before the doctor asked for their attention. Chad looked up and around the room.

Dr. Jones looked at Chad. "So this girl, she's your daughter?"

"You even have to ask?"

"Officially, yes."

"Yes, this is our Macy. I was there when she was born. I would know her anywhere."

"Have you ever seen Heather before?"

Chad looked over at the other girl. "No, but she looks so much like Macy. I don't understand."

Macy sat up. "Chester—her dad—he found me online. He was looking for someone who looked just like Heather and he pretended to be a boy so I would meet with him. He wanted me to replace her since he lost custody of her."

"He killed my mom," Heather said. "Do you believe me now? He's crazy enough to kidnap someone to replace me. He killed my mom." Tears fell down her face. "She's not in Paris. She's not."

Dr. Jones frowned. "Your story is more believable now, Heather. We need to look into it, because we've talked with your mom."

"He found someone to replace me. You think he couldn't have found someone to pretend to be Mom over the phone?"

"Like I said, we'll look into it. Right now, we need to focus on one thing at a time. Once we get Macy's situation squared away, we'll figure out what's going on with you. Like I told you before, your dad is being questioned right now."

"I hope they lock him up forever."

"Me too," Macy said.

Dr. Jones looked at Macy. "Once you identify him as your kidnapper, he'll be arrested. He should be put away for years for that alone. If it turns out that he also killed his wife, let's hope he'll be sentenced for life."

Chad looked over at Fleshman and Anderson, who were both furiously taking notes.

Fleshman looked at Macy. "I know this will be difficult, but we need you to tell us everything."

"Wh…where do you want me to start?"

"From the first time you came into contact with Chester Woodran."

Macy shook and Chad pulled her close. "Mom and I are here, baby. I promise you won't get into trouble for a single thing. Tell them everything."

Chad listened in disbelief as Macy told her entire story, starting from the boy who started chatting with her on social media, showing her attention that no one else had. His heart broke into more pieces than before as she described everything the madman had done to his daughter.

Finally, he couldn't take it anymore. He glared at Fleshman. "Are you going to arrest that dirt bag yet or what?"

"Chad, let her finish the story. We can't proceed until we've taken her full statement."

"Go on, honey." Chad kissed the top of her head again.

Macy continued her story, telling the story of being taken to a cult. Chad wanted to interrupt and ask questions, but he knew there would time for that later. He pulled her closer. How would he ever let her go again?

"Wait," Fleshman said. "A cult? Where's it located?"

"Yeah," Macy said. "It's in the mountains. I don't really know where."

"That's fine. We'll talk to you more about that later. Maybe the body and the kidnapping are related."

Macy stared at the officers. "There are other kidnapped kids there in the community. You guys have to get there and take them home, too." She went on to explain what life was like there and then she told the story of her escape attempt. Her eyes filled with tears as she talked about Luke and Dorcas. When she told of Chester shooting Dorcas, Macy dissolved into tears, pushing her face into Chad's chest once again. He held her tight as she soaked his shirt with tears.

Heather stood up. "See? Dad killed a girl—just a kid! He didn't even think twice about it. He just did it. Why wouldn't he kill Mom? She probably wanted a divorce and he did away with her. He killed her. Will you listen to me now? Please!"

Dr. Jones nodded. "Sit down, Heather. I'm sure that your dad is going to be locked away for a long, long time. We need to focus on one thing at a time."

"Make sure Mom's death is on his list of offenses." Heather sat, crossing her arms.

"Macy, can you tell us the rest of the story? From what you've described, that was around the new year. What happened since then?"

Sniffing, Macy sat up. She looked into Chad's eyes. The look on her face broke Chad. New tears fell from his own eyes.

"Daddy, it's my fault that Dorcas died. It's all my fault."

"No. No, baby. It's not your fault. Chester's the one who pulled the trigger."

"But if I hadn't snuck out of the house, we never would have gone there. If I hadn't insisted on getting out of the community that night, she'd still be alive. It's my fault." She fell against him again.

Alyssa leaned over, rubbing Macy's back. "You did nothing wrong, honey. You were just trying to get away."

Macy nodded, her face still against Chad.

Officer Anderson came over to them and put his face near Macy's. "Macy, dear, listen to me. I'm a police officer and from everything you've told me, you have nothing to feel guilty about. All of this is on Chester. He's the one who lured you, kidnapped you, took you there, and shot the girl. He did it all. You did the right thing by trying to get away."

Macy sat up. "But it's still my fault."

Anderson shook his head. "No, honey, it's not."

Dr. Jones looked at Chad. "You're going to have to get her into counseling when you get back home. She can't walk around with that false guilt."

"We know that," Alyssa said. She continued to run her hands through Macy's hair. "Can you tell us the rest of the story, baby? What happened next?"

"But first you guys have to find Luke. He's missing and he probably needs help. I'm sure of it. I hope he didn't go back to the community. They might have...." Macy's eyes filled with tears again.

Rage ran through Chad as Macy told them about Chester breaking her leg. If the police didn't arrest Chester and put him on death row, Chad would find a way to kill the bastard with his own two hands.

He held her even tighter as he listened to her tell the rest of the story of how she was forced to cook and clean for the psychos. It was all he could to stay silent. Macy held it together remarkably well. He didn't know how she did it.

When she was done talking, she collapsed against him. He kissed the top of her head again.

Alyssa spoke up. "Are you guys going to arrest that man now? You've just made Macy relive every horrible moment of her ordeal."

"Her testimony is going to make a huge difference. We need to hear what Heather has to say about him too," Fleshman said.

"You don't have enough on him from what Macy said? He kidnapped her and did all those awful things to her against her will. He nearly killed her, too!"

"We have plenty, but we need to know the whole story. Heather's been trying to tell her side for a long time. We need to give her some floor space as well."

Dr. Jones squirmed in his seat, looking uncomfortable.

Chad looked over at Heather, still unable to get over how much she looked like his daughter. She looked like she had been through a lot, too, forced to stay in this hospital for even longer than Macy had been missing.

"What about everything she's been through?" Chad asked. "She's been locked up in here with no one listening to her. That's not right." He glared at the doctor. "Who was looking out for her? Seems to me the hospital should have to answer for that. Maybe if they would have listened, Macy could have been spared what she went through—or at least some of it."

Anderson nodded. "It'll be investigated thoroughly, I assure you." He turned to Heather. "Tell us your story, please."

Light

MACY WALKED OUTSIDE with her parents, blinking fast in the bright light. She still couldn't believe that it was really happening. She was free. And Chester had been arrested.

One of the police men who had been taking notes asked her dad if he wanted them to drive their car home.

"No. I can do it. Thanks for everything, you guys." He shook both of their hands. "When everyone else wanted us to give up, you kept helping us. We can't possibly thank you enough."

Macy looked back inside the building where Heather stood with some other officers. They were supposed to take her to the farm to stay with Chester's parents. What would they think when they found out Macy hadn't been Heather?

Heather caught Macy's stare and gave a little wave. Macy waved back. They were both going to be okay. Macy more than her, since she was going back home to her parents and brother.

"Come on, honey," said her mom.

Macy looked at her parents and followed them to her dad's car. She felt a strange joy well up inside of her. Not only was the car familiar, but it was going to take her back home. She would be able to sleep in her own bed, wear her own clothes, and hopefully sleep a lot.

Her dad opened the back door for her. He smiled, but tears shone in his eyes. Macy wrapped him in a hug. "I'm so sorry for everything, Dad. I—"

"Shh. Just get in the car. We're glad to have you back. No more talk about the past. Not now." He kissed the top of her head.

"Okay." She climbed in and breathed deeply. It smelled just like home. She leaned her head against the back of the seat and closed her eyes. As soon as she relaxed, she expected to hear Chester's voice. She sat up gasping.

"Are you okay?" her mom asked, turning around.

"Yeah. Sorry." It would it take a while to get used to being back at home.

"Do you need anything?" her dad asked. "Are you hungry? We can stop somewhere and get you any vegan meal you want. I saw sub shop by the freeway."

Macy shrugged. Her nerves had her stomach twisting in knots. "Maybe later. I kinda just want to get home. How's Alex?"

Her parents exchanged one of their looks.

"What?" Macy asked.

"You wouldn't believe how much he's missed you." Her dad started the car. "I've never seen a brother who loves his sister more."

Alyssa turned around again. "He was the one who figured out that you were gone that first morning. He hasn't stopped worrying about you since. None of us have."

"What about Zoey? Have you seen her?"

Her mom had a funny look on her face. "Yeah. She's been spending a lot of time with us. She and Alex have gotten close."

"Yeah, they've always been like siblings, too."

They didn't say anything, so Macy looked out the window. "Can I talk to him?" she asked.

"To Alex?" her mom asked.

"Yeah."

She handed Macy her phone.

Macy stared at it, nervous. Her throat closed up and new tears stung at her eyes. "I can't." She handed the phone back, sniffing. "I'd better wait until I see him. How long will that be?"

"It's a few hours."

Macy didn't want to wait that long, but she would rather give him a big hug before saying anything. "Okay. Mind if I sleep? I know you probably want to catch up, but I'm exhausted."

Her mom smiled at her. "If you need rest, baby, get some sleep. After everything you've been through, I wouldn't be surprised if you slept for days."

"Yeah, honey," her dad said. "Don't worry about anything other than taking care of yourself."

"Thanks." She grabbed a coat and turned it into a makeshift pillow. As she leaned against it, she smelled her dad's cologne. She took a deep breath and smiled. Everything was going to be okay. She would get back home and everything would go back to the way it had been. She drifted off to sleep thinking about everything in her house.

Her mom's voice woke her up. Macy sat up, groggy. "What?"

"We're getting close."

Macy stretched and looked out the window. She recognized everything. They were about five minutes from home.

"Alex and Zoey are thrilled to see you. They're over at Zoey's now, but I let them know we're almost home."

Macy couldn't find any words. They pulled into the neighborhood and before she knew it, they pulled into their driveway and then into the garage.

"We don't want the neighbors swarming you," her dad said. "Everyone has been looking for you." He pushed a button on the visor, closing the garage door.

"That was nice of them." Macy yawned and then got out of the car. She looked around the garage, never so happy to see it. Everything looked exactly as she remembered it. They went inside and Macy continued to take everything in. It was all comfortably familiar, yet felt new at the same time. The house had the same maple scent it always did. Her mom loved those air fresheners.

They made their way up the stairs and as she scanned the front room, she saw Alex standing in front of Zoey. Macy's feet took off from under her and she ran into Alex's arms, causing him to stumble. He wrapped his arms around her. He shook. Was he actually crying? Macy looked into his eyes, and sure enough, tears were spilling out.

"Look at you," Macy said, through her own tears. She backed up a little. "You've really gotten bigger. Look, you're taller than me now."

"You too. Well, taller than you were, I mean. And your hair. I like it."

He threw his arms around her again.

She squeezed him tight. "I've missed you so much, Alex."

"Me too. I never thought I'd see you again. I never gave up on you, but it was so long and everything. I can't believe you're actually here. Don't ever leave again, okay? You have to promise."

Macy smiled. "I'll do my best. I won't be sneaking out again, that's for sure."

"You'd better not. You'll have to deal with me if you do."

She gave him another squeeze. "I need to give Zoey a hug." Macy let go of Alex, almost needing to push him away because he wouldn't let go. She stared at Zoey before running into her arms. She looked different. More round in the face. Had she put on weight? Then she noticed her stomach. "Zoey! What happened? Well, I mean, I guess I know *what* happened. But, who...when...?"

Zoey smiled wide. "Shut up and give me a hug."

Macy gave her a soft hug, not wanting to injure her middle.

"Oh, come on. A real hug. You're not going to break me." Zoey squeezed Macy so tight she nearly choked.

"Why don't we give them some time?" her dad asked her mom.

Her mom nodded, taking his hand.

Macy's eyes popped wide. They were holding hands?

"We'll get some dinner ready," Macy's mom said, leaning against her dad.

"Sure." Macy shook her head. That would take some getting used to. Her parents had barely been able to be in the same room before she left.

The landline rang. Her dad sighed. "Looks like we're going to be fielding calls again."

Her mom's cell phone rang. "At least we have good news this time." They went upstairs.

Macy turned to Zoey. "You've got to tell me everything. Do you have a boyfriend?"

Zoey bit her lip and looked away. "Yeah, kinda."

"Kind of?" Macy asked.

"You might wanna sit," Zoey said.

"I've been sitting for the last three hours. I'd rather not. Can we go up to my room, and you can tell me on the way? I'm dying to see my stuff."

"You've got to tell us everything," Alex said. "I've had all these images running through my head. I want the truth—I need to get rid of the fake stuff. Dad said you were kidnapped, but that's all we know. What happened?"

Macy headed for the stairs. "I'll tell you everything in my room."

They followed her up to the bedroom. Macy threw herself on the bed and looked over at Ducky, who ran to the side of the cage and looked her way.

Zoey closed the door, but Alex opened it and went out.

"Where's he going?" Zoey asked.

"Does anything make sense that he does?" Macy asked, smiling. She sat up. "You have no idea how good it is to be back home."

"And you have no idea how great it is to have you back."

"Looks like you kept yourself occupied, though."

"Well, I was stressed about you being gone."

"You don't have to explain yourself. I hardly expected anyone to stop their life just because I wasn't there."

Zoey's eyes narrowed. "Well, that's what happened. Everyone was crushed. There were times I could barely breathe. You should've seen your parents and Alex. You wouldn't believe how upset Alex was. He's been in counseling for the longest time. He could barely function."

"Really?"

"Your brother loves you. Never doubt that, no matter how big of dork he's being."

Alex came in. "Who's a dork?"

"You," Zoey said.

"That figures." He handed Macy her diaries. "I was looking for clues to find you. Hope you're not mad that I read them."

Macy shook her head. "How could I be? Though we might have to talk later about how you knew where they were."

Alex's cheeks turned red. "We don't have to."

"It's so good to be back." Macy leaned against her headboard. "I never thought I'd get back home." She looked at Zoey's stomach again. "Are you going to keep changing the subject or are you going to tell me who the guy is?"

"You're looking at him," Alex said.

Macy stared at her brother for a moment before the reality of what he said hit her. "You mean…?"

Alex nodded. His face was somewhat squished together, like he was nervous or something. "I guess we had a funny way of dealing with our grief."

"Sorry, Macy," Zoey said. She also looked worried. "I know he's your brother. I hope you're not mad. I never meant to drag him into this."

Alex shook his head. "You didn't drag me into anything. I—"

"So, are you two together-together or was it, like, a one-time thing?" Macy felt light-headed.

Zoey grabbed Alex's hand. "We're together. We're in love."

"Oh." Macy never would have guessed they would have liked each other like that. She watched as they both looked back and forth between her and each other. It would take some getting used to, but it would probably be cool.

"Are you okay with us?" Zoey asked.

"As long as I'm not the third wheel, I guess so. It's going to take some getting used to, but I can't complain. Not after everything I've been through. I'm alive and home with you guys. I couldn't ask for anything more."

"Third wheel?" Alex asked. "Not a chance." He gave her a huge hug, nearly knocking her off the bed.

"Yeah, no way," Zoey added. "We're never letting you out of our sight, so you'd better get used to us being around."

"I can handle that." Macy smiled.

"Now we just need to find a guy for you," Zoey said.

"Don't look for a thirteen year old. I'm not—"

"Hey!" Zoey laughed. "Are you making fun of me?"

"Maybe."

"Where should we look, then?"

"Oh, I'm in no hurry to get a boyfriend."

Zoey's face got serious again. "Because of what you've been through?"

"There's that, but I kind of have one. I just have to find him."

"What? You mean Jared?"

"No. Jared was a lie." Macy's eyes got misty. "I met someone while I was away, but it…we got separated."

"What do you mean?" Zoey tilted her head. It was obvious that she knew there was more to the story.

"Can I tell you about Luke later? I need to get used to being back home first."

Zoey took one of Macy's hands. "Anything you need. Just tell us, and it's yours. Got it? We'll do anything for you. At least, I will."

"Me too," Alex said. He pushed Zoey aside and gave Macy another hug.

Macy's throat felt like it was going to close up. Tears of happiness threatened.

Not only was she home, she was the luckiest girl alive.

Frenzy

A LEX WATCHED AS Macy walked to her window and looked outside. She turned to Alex. "Why are there so many vans outside?"

He took a deep breath, preparing himself to explain how the media had forced their way into their lives. He walked over and looked. "It the media circus."

The doorbell rang again, proving his point. It had been ringing for about a half an hour.

"What do you mean?" Macy looked out again. "But why are they here?"

"When you were first gone, they wouldn't leave us alone. There was always someone out there, ready to ask us questions if we went outside. For the longest time, a van was parked across the street just recording our house."

"Why?"

"You were the most exciting thing on the news for a long time. It drove Mom and Dad crazy. It was annoying, but I thought it was a little funny. I mean, we were like stars or something. Only it really sucked because you were missing."

"Well, at least Zoey went home before all of this. She never would have made it down to her house. When will they leave?"

"Hopefully soon. They did eventually leave us alone. I think it helped that Dad used his blog to post updates. People could get the answers they wanted without watching the news. Plus with all the click-throughs or whatever, he was able to stop working."

Macy leaned against the wall. "Things have really changed, haven't they?"

"Yeah, but everything will go back to normal."

"You think? You and Zo are going to have a baby. That feels weird to even say."

"When we were at the appointment, her parents were talking about raising her."

"Her? It's a girl?"

Alex's lips curled slightly and his heart rate picked up. "Yeah, we found out today. It's been a huge day. You came back and we found out the baby's a girl."

"So, now that Zoey's dad is here, her parents are getting back together?"

"Yep. It's weird. They haven't seen each other in fifteen years and now they want to be family. I think he feels guilty."

"Are Mom and Dad okay with them raising the baby?" asked Macy.

"Not that it's their decision, but they don't want to raise a baby, and they don't want me ruining my life to raise her either, so I'm sure they'll be happy. We can see her whenever we want. Zoey and me are together all the time anyway."

"I don't know if I'll ever get used to that. Are you guys still…? Ew."

Alex's face became warm. "It's not gross. It's—"

"I don't wanna hear about it. Sorry I asked. What did Mom and Dad say when they found out?"

"Do we have to talk about this?" Alex squirmed.

Macy smiled and poked him. "I thought guys liked to brag about doing it."

"Not me, and you're my sister. It's just weird, you know? What about that Luke guy? Did you guys…?"

Sadness covered her face, and he immediately regretted asking.

Macy shook her head. "No. He gave me a kiss, though." She explained about the community and their escape.

Alex's heart felt like it had been ripped out of his chest. He put his arm around her. "I'm sure they'll find him."

Macy turned to look Alex in the eyes. Tears fell from her eyes and she put her head on Alex's shoulders. "You think so?"

"Why not? He sounds strong and capable. Besides, I want to see the guy who won you over."

They stood there like that for a while. Time either stood still or rushed by; Alex couldn't tell. He was just glad to have Macy back.

The bedroom door opened and he turned to see his mom.

"Is everything okay?" she asked.

Alex shrugged. "We were just talking. Did she tell you about Luke?"

"Oh, baby. Don't think about him." She came over and wrapped her arms around both of them. "Focus on being home. We want you to relax and unwind."

"I can't forget about everything, Mom."

"Honey, I'm not asking you to forget. Hey, do you want to see your picture on TV? You're all over the news."

"I am?"

Alex wasn't surprised, but that might the distraction his sister needed. "Yeah. You're practically a celeb. Come and see."

Macy shrugged. "Okay."

They went into the bonus room, where the news was already on. A picture of Macy from their dad's blog flashed on the screen. The word *Found* flashed underneath. Alex watched Macy. He couldn't tell what she was thinking.

When a dog food commercial came on, he asked, "What do you think of that?"

"It's weird to watch the news again."

"You haven't watched any TV?"

"Well, I saw some ancient reruns at the farmhouse, but that was months ago. It was before the community. I saw part of a movie yesterday at the mental hospital."

Farmhouse? Mental hospital? Alex shook his head. "You'll have to tell me about that later."

The doorbell rang.

"When will it stop?" Macy asked.

"Probably when Dad gets mad enough to scream at them," Alex said.

"Where is Dad?" Macy asked.

"Probably updating the blog. Once he gives everyone what they want, hopefully they'll leave us alone. That's worked before."

His mom shook her head. "I'm not so sure that'll work this time around. They're going to want to see Macy for themselves. Everyone is going to want to interview her. I suspect this could be worse than before."

Alex groaned. "They need to leave her alone! Don't they know she needs to relax and stuff? I'll go out there and—"

"Let Dad deal with them, Alex."

"Fine, but if they don't give her the space she needs, I can't guarantee anything." He scowled.

Macy's picture flashed on the screen. The newscaster spoke about where she had been found and then Chester's face appeared in the opposite corner of Macy's.

Alex noticed Macy tense up.

"Is that the guy?" Alex asked.

"That's Chester."

"Did he ever say why he took you?"

"Alex," his mom said in a warning tone, "she doesn't want to talk about it now."

"I don't mind, Mom." She told him about Heather and her mom.

"What a sick jerk," Alex said. "They'd better lock him away for a long time. If they ever let him out, I'll—"

"Alex, he has a lot of charges against him," his mom said. "I wouldn't worry about him getting out."

"He'd better not." Alex clenched his fists and stared at the picture of his sister's abductor. "He doesn't look like someone who would do all that. He's a nerd. Look at those glasses and that hair. He looks like someone who gets beat up, not someone who kidnapped someone and killed two people."

Macy sighed. "That's just it. He was picked on his whole life. I guess he just snapped. That's what it sounds like, anyway."

"Maybe there was a reason people bullied him. He doesn't deserve to live," Alex said.

"Honey—"

"No, Mom. It's the truth. He's a waste of space. I hope he gets a death sentence."

"We'll let the jury decide that."

"Whatever." Alex looked back and forth between the TV and his sister. Even though he'd been talking with her, it still didn't feel real yet. He kept waiting to wake up—in his bed, alone.

Macy caught him looking at her. She gave him a slight smile and took his hand. "I really missed you."

His throat closed up and tears stung at his eyes. "Me, too. You have no idea."

She squeezed his hand, her eyes shining with tears.

"Oh, you guys," Alyssa gushed. She wrapped them both in a hug. She pulled back and stared at Macy. "I hope you know I'm never letting you out of my sight."

"That's fine by me," Macy said. "I don't want to go anywhere ever again."

"That's good," Alex said, "because people are going to be all over you when you do leave the house. The news didn't leave us alone for a long time after you disappeared."

"What about school?" Macy asked. "Don't we have to go to school?"

"Zoey and I have been homeschooling."

Macy's eyes widened. "Why?"

Alex shrugged. "I couldn't really focus, plus I had to deal with all the things those jerks said."

"What do you mean? People have always been nice to you."

Anger burned in his chest. "They were saying things like you were dead. Had it gone much longer, I would have been expelled for beating kids up."

"And Zoey? Because of the baby?"

"Honey," Alyssa said, "we've all been beside ourselves with grief and worry. Life never just picked up where it left off. Dad couldn't keep working either. Luckily he had the blog to fall back on."

"Wait!" Macy said, looking at the TV. "I want to see this."

Alex looked at the screen and saw police busting down a large wooden gate in what appeared to be a forest.

"They're going to get the other kidnapped kids," Macy said. Her hand tightened around Alex's. He had forgotten she still held onto his hand.

The fence finally fell to the ground and the officers rushed in. People in white ran around, looking scared. Women with tight buns grabbed children and ran into little buildings. Men jumped on horses and ran off.

"You were *there?*" Alex asked. "The dude who kidnapped you was Amish?"

Macy shook her head. "Shh."

The screen faded away and then showed several people handcuffed and being taken into the police cruisers.

"Did you know them?" Alex asked.

"Those are the leaders. I bet Jonah didn't see *that* in his visions," Macy said, her voice dripping with sarcasm.

"What?" asked Alyssa.

"Never mind. Look. They're taking some kids. I hope they get to go back to their families, too."

"Was it weird talking with other kids who had been abducted?" Alyssa asked.

Macy shrugged. "We didn't really get to talk like that. It was forbidden to talk about life outside the community. Everyone was even given new names."

Alyssa's eyes widened. "What was your name?"

"We weren't there long enough, so everyone knew me as Heather."

"Heather?" Alex asked. "Oh, right. That d-bag's daughter."

Macy still hadn't taken her eyes off the screen.

"Are you looking for Luke?" Alex asked.

"Yeah. I haven't seen him. I don't know if that's good or bad."

"I'm sure he's safe," Alex said.

"Wait," Macy exclaimed. "There he is. That's him and his mom talking to some cops by that car right there." Macy jumped up and pointed. "That's Luke." Tears shone in her eyes.

"The police will make sure he's taken care of," said her mom, wrapping an arm around Macy. She kissed her forehead.

Macy shook. "I need to talk with him. We have to find him."

"We will."

Macy stared at the TV screen which was no longer on Luke or his mom. "You think we'll be able to find them?"

"The policemen who were with us when we found you, they'll help us however they can."

"I hope so," Macy said. She shook, staring at the television.

Returned

M ACY FELT SOMETHING brush against her cheek, and she rolled over covering her face with the blankets. Something pushed on her leg. She pulled it close and tucked it under her arms.

"Time to wake up, Heather."

Macy's eyes popped open. What was Chester's voice doing at home? Wasn't she home? Had it all been a too-realistic dream?

"Heather, don't ignore me."

Her heart pounded in her ears.

"Don't evade me, or there's going to be trouble. You know what that means, don't you?"

Macy sat up, ready to claw his face. "Get out of my room."

"You're going to pay for everything you've done. How dare you run away from me? Try to get me into trouble? They're looking for your mom and questioning me. We have to leave before they arrest me."

"I'll scream, Chester. My family's just down the hall. They'll come, and then you will go back to jail."

Chester shook his head slowly. "That's where you're wrong, dear Heather. We don't have to worry about them anymore. Remember what I told you would happen if you ever ran away?"

The blood drained from Macy's face. "You didn't."

He held up a bloody butcher knife. "Now we don't have to worry about them any more. None of them. Come on, your true family awaits."

Tears streamed down her face. "You're lying."

Chester held the knife close and smelled it. "There's nothing like the smell of fresh blood. You want to know what your family's blood smells like?"

Macy screamed.

"I wouldn't do that if I were you."

She screamed even louder.

"Heather...."

"If they can't hear you, then the neighbors will. There are cops across the street."

"I took care of them, too. We have nothing standing in our way now. It's time to go home and be a family forever. I've even convinced Jonah and the prophets to forgive everything. Of course, you'll have to be under strict watch, but we can go back, and everything will be the same as it was. As it's meant to be."

"No. I won't go with you. You'll have to kill me too."

"That would break my heart, Heather."

Macy thought about telling him the real Heather was out of the hospital, but she wouldn't be able to live with herself if Heather had to go back to him.

"You won't take me again."

He grabbed her arm, pulling her out of bed. "You're wrong again."

"I'll scream louder." Macy dug her nails into his skin. "Let go of me."

"Your yelling didn't help you a minute ago, did it?" He yanked her arm.

Macy pushed her nails in farther. His blood escaped, dripping onto her fingers. "You like blood so much, there you go."

He held the knife to her throat. "I'll kill you slowly and painfully like I did them. You should have heard your dad and brother. They both cried like sissies."

"Liar." Macy screamed again, taking all the energy she had.

"Macy." That was her mom's voice.

She looked around for her mom. "Mom, where are you?"

"You're hearing things," Chester said. "I killed her, too. Come with me."

"Macy, wake up." That was her brother.

"Alex!" she screamed. "Stay away from him, you guys!"

Someone shook her from behind. "Wake up, Macy! Wake up."

"I can't see you." Macy shook as Chester pressed the knife into her flesh. "Get away," she begged.

"You need to wake up, Macy," said her dad.

"Where are you guys? Are you ghosts?" Macy looked around.

"Of course they're ghosts," Chester said. "They're angry I won. We're going back to the community, and you'll never leave it again. You won't embarrass me, and you'll always do as I say."

Macy shook her head. "Never. Not again. You'll have to kill me first."

"You keep saying that like I would actually do it. You'd like that, wouldn't you? Then you could be with those people you keep calling family. Don't you get it? I'm your family. You, me, Rebekah, and the baby."

"Just kill me. Please."

"Macy, open your eyes."

"Where are you, Mom?" Macy asked, looking around.

Chester pressed the tip of the knife harder against her neck. Then he turned her chin toward him. "You need to forget about them. Like you said, they're ghosts. You can't come back here again. There's no one to come to. We need to get home. Some of the puritans are getting our house ready as we speak.

"Macy, you have to wake up," cried Alex.

"Alex, are you real?"

"Stop talking to ghosts, you stupid girl." Chester squeezed her cheeks, staring at her through those big, ugly glasses that Macy hated so much. "If you don't stop this nonsense, you're going to make me mad. I'll lose my temper. You don't want that, do you? We can stop by Grandma and Grandpa's farm. How does that sound?"

Macy screamed, and then she hit and kicked him. She didn't even care if he pushed the knife in and killed her. She wasn't going to go anywhere with him, much less back to the community.

Something cold and wet covered her face. She looked at Chester, but his hands were on her and the knife.

Even though her eyes were open, she opened them again. Macy blinked and sat up in her bed. How had she gotten back in there? She looked around, gasping for air. Where was Chester?

Her mom, dad, and brother stood around the bed staring at her, looking as scared as she felt.

"I told you the cold washcloth would work," Alex said.

"Where did he go? Did he kill me? Am I a ghost now too?" Macy looked around. "We have to get away from him. He—"

Her dad wrapped his arms around her, holding her tight. "Shh, baby. You're safe. It was only a dream."

Macy shook her head. "No, it was real. He was here. Chester had a bloody knife. He said he killed you all, and I had to go back with him. It was—"

"It wasn't real, honey," her dad said. "You're home, and we're all here. No one's going to take you away from us again."

Macy struggled to catch her breath.

"Do you want to tell us about the dream?" her mom asked. "Anytime you want to talk about anything—anything at all—we're all here for you. Unlike before, we'll listen. We'll hear you out without interrupting."

Alex grabbed her hand. "You're not going anywhere, and neither are we. In fact, you're stuck with us. You couldn't get rid of us if you wanted."

"I hope so." Macy went limp in her dad's arms. She gasped for air until she was breathing normally. Then she sat up and looked at all of them. "Why don't you guys go back to bed? I don't want to keep you up."

Her mom shook her head. "We're not going anywhere. Sleep means nothing now that you're back. We're here for you anytime you need us."

Tears filled Macy's eyes. "I'm so sorry I ever snuck out. I'm so sorry."

"We're sorry we wouldn't listen to you," her dad said.

Alex squeezed her hand. "And I'm sorry I teased you and didn't beat up all those kids who bullied you. That's what I should have done. I was a horrible brother, but now things are different."

Macy shook her head. "You weren't a bad brother. I know you were just trying to cheer me up."

He frowned. "Well, I was stupid."

Her mom looked into her eyes. "Do you want to talk about your nightmare?"

"No. I just want to forget about everything I went through. I'm home now. I guess I just have to get used to that."

"Do you want to go back to sleep?" her dad asked.

Macy thought about it. Her dreams were the one place where Chester could still hunt her down. "No. I think I'll check my emails or something. I probably have a ton."

"I have a better idea," her mom said. "Why don't we have another family movie night? You and Alex pick something to watch while Dad and I get snacks? How does popcorn, ice cream, candy, and pop sound?"

"Like a dream come true," Macy said.

Her dad stood up and helped her out of bed. "A middle of the night movie it is. Let's get the snacks, Lyss." He took her hand and they looked into each other's eyes.

Warmness filled Macy as she watched them. She looked over at Alex and he smiled.

"You two better hurry," said their mom, "because if you don't have a movie picked out by the time we get there, we'll pick out something."

"And you probably won't like it," her dad teased.

Alex and Macy exchanged a look.

"Don't you dare," Alex said. He grabbed Macy's arm and they ran to the bonus room together.

Macy walked over to the shelf and saw several DVD's that still had the shrink wrap. She grabbed a comedy that she had wanted to see before she was kidnapped. It felt like she had picked that out years earlier. "You guys never watched any of these?"

"Are you kidding?" Alex asked.

Macy's shoulders drooped. "I'm so sorry. I never should have—"

"Let's make an agreement. No more saying sorry for anything that happened before. I think we all have lots to be sorry for, but we should just move on instead."

"Yeah. You're right. We should—"

"Snacks are here," said their mom. Both of their parents came into the room with their arms full.

Macy and Alex exchanged an excited look. Their parents never let them eat all that junk food.

Her dad handed Macy a small bowl of popcorn. "This one has no butter."

"I don't care about being vegan anymore." She gave the bowl of butterless popcorn to Alex and grabbed the big tub from her dad.

"You think you're going to eat all that?" Alex teased.

"I might think about sharing. Maybe." Macy smiled.

Alyssa put everything in her arms on the coffee table. "What movie are we watching?"

Macy picked up the comedy. "I hope this is okay."

"It's perfect."

Alex took it from Macy and ripped the plastic off and threw it on the floor. Macy looked over at her mom, waiting for her to tell Alex to throw it away. Her mom shrugged and then pulled Macy into a hug. "I can't tell you how good it is to have you back."

"And I can't tell you how happy I am to be back. I can't believe how much has changed. You and Dad look happy."

"We've had some stuff to work through, and it did get rough for a while, but in the end we pulled together for you."

Macy hugged her back.

"Where's the DVD remote?" Alex asked.

"Use the universal," Macy said.

"The batteries died months ago. We've just been using the main remote since we've only watched the news."

Alex found the remote and turned the TV on. Chester's face showed up on the screen.

Macy choked on popcorn. Her mom whacked her back until it came free.

"Turn that off," her dad told Alex.

"No. Listen," Alex said.

The picture of Chester shrunk, and the newscaster came into view in front of a prison. "To recap: Chester Woodran is now under investigation for the murder of his wife. After a search of his home, journals were found detailing the location of his missing wife and how he allegedly killed her. The diaries also further proved his intent to kidnap Macy Mercer. Authorities are at the scene of the alleged burial spot now. We haven't been given the location yet."

Macy's heart pounded in her chest as she stood staring at the screen.

"I thought he was going to get away with that," she whispered.

"In those journals," continued the newscaster, "Was also evidence of the murder of a teen who had been part of this commune. Her body was said to have been left in Clearview, and was somehow connected to a fire in a building used by dentists and orthodontists. Authorities are looking into this also. New updates will be available as soon we learn more."

"It's over. It's really over," Alex said.

Macy's parents both put their arms around her.

"It really is," her mom said. "Now we can all focus on healing."

"And we can start with this movie," Alex said, switching over to the DVD player.

They sat down together on the couch, munching on sugary, buttery goodness as Macy's heart returned to normal. She looked around as the movie started. She was pretty sure she had never been happier in all her life.

Time

ZOEY LAUGHED, WATCHING Alex and Macy chase each other with squirt guns. She wanted to join them, but she could barely walk—it was more of a waddle—so there was no way she could join them. Probably next year.

"Go, Macy!" she called.

"Hey," Alex said, giving her a mock upset look. It was obvious he was going easy on his sister.

Macy turned around and soaked him.

Alex looked back to Zoey. "Thanks for the distraction. Did you two have that planned?"

"You know it." Zoey picked up her glass of ice water and took a drink. Was it getting even hotter? She leaned back into the lawn chair and fanned herself. Her stomach tightened. The baby must be stretching out. There was no room in there, and her skin couldn't stretch any more.

Alyssa sat next to her. "How are you doing, Zoey?"

"It's too hot."

"I'm not even pregnant and I agree. Can I get you anything?"

"A new body?"

Alyssa patted Zoey's knee. "Soon enough. Think you'll make your due date?"

"The doctor says she can come anytime two weeks before or after the date and it's still on time."

"You're only a week away."

"I know." Zoey repositioned herself. Her legs were going numb. "Will my feet go back to normal?"

"Sure they will. My feet swelled too, but I always went back to wearing my old shoes."

"Man, I hope so. I can't believe I had to buy flip flops two sizes too big—and they fit." Zoey frowned, ignoring her stomach tightening again. The baby was sure being active. "Is it true first babies are usually late?"

"Each one is different. A first can be early and the second can be late. No matter what, they like to keep us on our toes."

Zoey nodded.

"Let me get you some more water. Or do you want to come inside? It's cooler in there."

Her entire body ached and nothing sounded better than a nap, but Zoey didn't want to move. She handed Alyssa her glass and closed her eyes. She listened to Macy and Alex shrieking at each other. It was good to have Macy back and have things returning to normal. It had taken a while for Macy to become herself again. At first, every time she heard a noise she would jump. Now, not so much.

Zoey's stomach tightened again. This time she held her breath. Maybe it wasn't the baby moving around. It was more of a squeezing sensation— like her body was getting ready to push. A contraction? It couldn't be. She'd been feeling the tightening for months, although not as intense as it was right then.

It stopped and she relaxed. She opened her eyes and saw Macy and Alex helping Chad put meat and veggie burgers on the grill. Alex looked over at her and smiled. Zoey waved back. Alex turned back to his dad and spread sauce over the grill contents. Her eyes grew heavy, and just as she was about to give into them, Alyssa handed her a full glass of ice water.

"Thanks." She drank most of it and set it on a tray next to her.

Alyssa went over to the grill and Zoey looked up into the sky and watched a few small clouds. There was a painful kick in her ribs—that was the baby. She grimaced, waiting for more, but it was the just the one. Then her stomach tightened so painfully that she sat up. She couldn't even get a sound out. Beads of sweat formed along her face.

When the pain finally stopped, she leaned back against the chair, catching her breath. Should she tell someone? The Mercers all looked so happy to be together. They were hungry and getting ready to eat. Zoey could let them enjoy their meal and then ask Alyssa if what she was feeling was contractions. Her water hadn't broke, so she had to be fine.

Alex came over. "Do you want ketchup on your...are you okay?"

Zoey nodded. "Fine."

He sat on the chair next to her. "Are you sure? You're sweating."

"It's hot and I've got two people's body heat."

"I know, but you look...not right."

"Just eat."

"Aren't you hungry?"

"There's hardly any room in my stomach." She closed her eyes.

She felt Alex's lips on her forehead. "If you need anything, let me know."

"All right." Zoey felt something similar to really bad cramps and then her stomach tightened again. Once that stopped, she felt nauseated along with severe lower back pain. She sat up in time to throw up on the lawn and not get anything on the chair.

Everyone ran over, asking if she was okay. Zoey stood up. "My back hurts so bad." A new wave of nausea swept over her, but she didn't throw up. A new wave hit and her stomach heaved. "I'm going to be sick again. Oh—" She turned away and threw up on her other pile.

Someone put their arms around her and guided her toward the house. Zoey stopped walking when her legs felt wet. She looked down saw the puddle around her feet on the deck. "I'm so sorry."

"Nothing to be sorry about," Alyssa said. She turned to Macy. "Call her parents."

Macy ran inside.

Alyssa turned to Alex. "Go inside and get some towels and clean clothes for Zoey."

He looked pale, but ran in also.

"Sorry to ruin your lunch," Zoey said.

Alyssa shook her head. "You have nothing to be sorry about. We'll get you cleaned up and then head to the hospital. Do you have a hospital bag packed?"

"Mom's got something in her car."

"Okay. One less thing to worry about. We'll just get you there. Do you feel like you have to throw up again?"

Zoey shook her head. Her stomach tightened again, and she grasped it.

"Where's Alex?" Alyssa asked.

Macy burst out the door. "Valerie says she'll meet us there unless we can't take her. She's leaving work now."

"We'll take her," Alyssa said. "It wouldn't make sense for her to come here. Get your brother. We need towels."

Macy gave Zoey a sympathetic look and ran back inside.

Zoey felt another gush of liquid. "How many times can water break?"

"Only once, but it doesn't always rush out at the same time. We'll have you sit on some towels in the car just in case."

"Okay." Zoey's head was spinning. The pain was horrendous—all of it—but it was actually nice to have the distraction. She was scared of giving birth.

Alex and Macy ran outside, both carrying towels. They wiped Zoey's legs and soon she was inside changing her clothes. After that everything was a blur. She was vaguely aware of being in the car on top of a pile of towels.

When they got to the hospital, her parents were already there, both looking nervous. They ran over as soon as they saw her, asking her more questions than she could focus on.

A nurse came out and led them to her room. She asked even more questions than Zoey's parents. She answered them the best she could. Being in the hospital made everything feel even more real. Soon the baby would be out, and hopefully the pain would stop.

Zoey went into the bathroom and put on a gown while the nurse spoke with her parents. Where were Alex and Macy?

She went back into the room and was led to the bed, where she was hooked up to all kinds of things. The nurse said she would get the doctor.

Her parents spoke over each other again.

"Can you guys get Macy and Alex? I want them here." Zoey looked around the room. "It's big enough for everyone."

Her mom took Zoey's hand. "Are you sure you want to give the baby up for us to raise? You can still change your mind, you know."

Zoey shook her head. "It's better for everyone. We'll still live in the same house, and I can keep going to school and everything. It's not like she's going anywhere. Besides, I always wanted a sister." She tried to smile. "I just never thought it would be like this."

A doctor came in. "Dr. Johnson is on her way, but in the meantime, I'm going to check you out, Zoey. Is that okay?"

Zoey nodded, and then her stomach tightened again. This time it was so painful, she couldn't help but yell out. Once it passed, the doctor asked her the same questions the nurse had already asked and logged into a tablet. Zoey answered them again and then he examined her.

"It looks like you're progressing fast." He rattled off something about centimeters and other stuff that meant nothing to Zoey.

She was waiting for the next wave of pain to hit. "Can I get some medicine?"

When he left, Zoey looked around and asked her dad, "Where's Mom?"

"She went to get Macy and Alex. Do you want me to leave? I understand if you do."

Zoey shrugged. "You're fine, Dad."

His face softened. She had never called him that before, and seeing the look on his face, she was glad she chose that moment.

He wrapped his arms around her. "Even though I haven't been around, I want you to know—"

Another round of pain struck and Zoey clutched her stomach, crying out in pain again. She was vaguely aware of him taking her hand. When the agony finally receded, Zoey opened her eyes.

Alex was next to her. He looked upset. "I'm so sorry, Zoey. I never meant to do this to you."

Family

MACY'S HEART POUNDED as she walked down the hospital hall with her parents and Zoey's parents. Even though she'd had some time to adjust to the thought of becoming an aunt, her heart continued to beat harder. That wasn't even the crazy part. Her baby brother was a dad now, even though he wasn't going to raise the baby.

The nurse opened a door on the left. "They're ready to see you. Go on inside."

Macy held her breath as she walked in. She let everyone else go in ahead of her. She was nervous, and she couldn't figure out why. Everyone in the room were the people she knew and loved most.

But it was different now. The baby changed everything. Her brother and best friend were parents. Her mom and dad were now grandparents. She looked at them, trying to grasp that. They definitely didn't look old enough.

The nurse moved aside a curtain. Macy saw Zoey in the bed with Alex next to her. She looked around her parents, wanting to see the baby. Everyone crowded around the bed, gasping about the baby.

Macy went around to the other side of the bed. Zoey held a tiny bundle with a little face poking out from the blanket. The eyes were closed, but she could tell the baby was beautiful.

She walked to Alex's side and gave him a hug. "How do you feel?"

"Too much. I'm proud and scared and overwhelmed. I'm glad that Zoey's parents are going to take care of her, because I would just mess her up."

Macy put her arm around him. "And you'll get to see her anytime you want."

He looked down at the baby. "I'm glad. Even though I know I'm too young to take care of her, I don't want her going far. I feel like I need to protect her."

Macy kissed his cheek, and then turned to Zoey. "How are you?"

"I just want to sleep for the next week, but I'm so sore. How are you, Auntie?"

"Better than you guys." Macy smiled.

Zoey handed her the bundle, and Macy sat down, afraid she'd do something to hurt the baby. "What's her name?"

"We're going to let Mom and Dad name her. They wanted to let me, but I think they should."

"Maybe you could pick the middle name."

"That's a great idea," Zoey's dad said. "What do you think, Zoey?"

"Alex and I could."

Macy got up and handed the baby to her mom and then stood near the bed, talking with Zoey and Alex. Zoey fell asleep mid-sentence and then Macy sat in a chair, tugging Alex to sit next to her.

They were quiet for a moment, listening to the adults talk. Zoey's parents assured hers they could all visit the baby anytime, and that they would honor them as the baby's grandparents. Macy's mom thanked them and said they would respect them as the parents.

Macy looked back over at Alex. He looked like he was going to fall asleep, too.

"Are you okay?" she asked him.

"I want to sleep for the next day too. Then you know what?"

"What?"

"I'm never having sex again."

Macy laughed. "Ever again?"

"Well, maybe not never. But it's going to be a long, long time."

"I'm sure Zoey feels the same way." Macy patted his hand.

"She was in so much pain, Macy."

Macy looked over at Zoey. "She's doing well now."

Alex ran his hands through his hair. "You didn't see her."

"She had a baby, Alex. It's not supposed to be easy."

"I don't ever want to do that to her again. Like I said, I'm never—"

"Don't make any rash decisions now. Besides, take another look at the baby. She's totally amazing."

"Yeah, I know. I can't explain how I felt when I first saw her."

"You guys made a whole new person, Alex. She wasn't here this morning and now she is. Don't feel too bad. Get some rest." Macy stood up, kissed the top of his head and went over to her dad who was holding the baby. "Can you believe how cute she is?"

Her dad smiled at her. "She looks a lot like you and Alex did as babies."

Macy looked at the little, sleeping face thinking back to her and Alex's baby pictures. She hadn't looked at them since before she was kidnapped, and that made it hard to remember. "I'll have to take your word on it, Dad. I was pretty young then."

She sat, listening to everyone talk for a while and grew drowsy.

Macy looked at Alex. "I'm going to get something with caffeine from a machine. Want to come with me?"

He shook his head. "I'm going to stay here with Zoey and the baby."

Macy kissed the top of his head, and then went out into the hall. She looked around trying to remember where she had seen the vending machines. Macy thought it had been to the left, so she went that way. Just as she was about to turn a corner, she heard a voice she would know anywhere. Rebekah.

She peeked around the corner, and sure enough Rebekah stood in the hall talking to some nurses. Her stomach was bigger than Zoey's had been, and she was talking with a nurse. An older man and woman were also with them.

"Are the babies okay?" asked the man. "We didn't know there were two. We couldn't even get her to come to a doctor until now."

The nurse looked at him. "They'll be fine. We just need to get her ready for the birth. It appears that we're going to need to break her water." The nurse looked at some papers. "I have here that she's not to be left alone because of psychological issues. What's the plan after being discharged from the hospital?"

"We're her parents, and she's staying at home with us. Between the two of us and her brother, she's never left alone. We're not letting her out of our sight until the psychologist gives us the okay."

The nurse scribbled notes on the paper. "I see something on her about an arrest warrant. We don't generally release—"

"As long as she stays under the care of her psychologist, she's able to avoid that. If she fully rehabilitates, they're going to remove that from her record," said Rebekah's dad. "The babies will be safe."

"Okay." The nurse scribbled more notes, and then they walked down the hall in the opposite direction as Macy.

She leaned against the wall, breathing heavily. As shocked as she was about having seen Rebekah, she was glad that she was at least getting counseling. Even though their relationship had ended strained, Macy would always be glad for the friendship Rebekah had shown her when Macy first moved into the community.

Surprise

MACY WAVED TO the receptionist at her counselor's office as she put her hand on the doorknob. "Bye, Shelley. See you next week."

"Have a good one, kiddo."

The sun was bright, so Macy dug into her purse and put on her sunglasses. "Good thing I parked in the shade," she muttered. She pulled out her cell phone and saw she had no missed calls or texts. "Looks like I have the afternoon to myself. The mall sounds like fun."

As Macy neared her car, she noticed someone leaning against her car. She groaned. The last thing she wanted was to deal with another reporter. She prepared herself to give a harsh answer—the only kind that would get rid of them—but she stopped cold when he turned around and looked at her.

His eyes shone brightly in the warm sun and the skin around his eyes crinkled as his lips formed a smile. "Hi, Macy."

"Luke, what are you doing here?" She ran into his arms, squeezing him tight.

He hugged her back. "I have the afternoon off. Thought I'd come by and see my favorite girlfriend."

"You mean your only girlfriend." Macy looked into his eyes, her lips forming a grin. "I'm so glad you did. Where's your car? I didn't see it anywhere, and it's not easy to miss."

Luke laughed. "No, she's not, is she? Mom took *The Beast* in for a tune up and dropped me off here. Hope you can give me a ride."

"I'll have to think about that." Macy paused, pretending to consider it.

"Or I can walk home. No big deal. See ya around." He turned around and took a couple steps.

"Get back here." She grabbed the back of his shirt.

"Yes, Ma'am." Luke spun around and placed his lips on top of hers. He smelled of aftershave. "Mind if we make a quick stop first? I have to drop something off for my mom."

"Sure." Macy unlocked the doors of her car with the remote and then climbed in. "Where to?"

"Near the corner of Third and Russell."

She started the car. "What's over there?"

Luke smiled, looking as gorgeous as possible. "Nothing exciting until you get there."

Macy's breath caught. She never got tired of looking at him. She pulled out of the parking spot. "Did you guys finally get the last of the boxes unpacked?"

"Yeah. It's great to be in our own place now. Renting that small room until we got on our feet was stressful."

"When do I get to come over and cook you guys a meal?"

"As soon as you want. I know my mom won't mind."

"Now that she's working full time finally, I'm sure she'd love the help."

"And I wouldn't mind the company." He elbowed her in the arm.

Macy nudged Luke back. "Watch out. I'll make you cook."

Luke laughed. "Don't make threats you don't intend to keep."

They continued to tease each other as Macy navigated the heavy afternoon traffic. It was summer, but this part of town always seemed congested.

"Okay," said Macy. "We're on Russell Street, and Third is coming up. Where do I turn?"

"There's supposed to be a turn right after we pass Third. Go right."

When she pulled into the parking lot, she looked at the nondescript little building. "What is this place?"

"Oh, some kind of hall or something. Want to come in with me?" He batted his eyelashes.

Her heart skipped a beat. Even though he was teasing, she couldn't help adoring him. "Anything for a little extra time with you."

They got out and Luke took her hand and they walked in the front door. It was dim inside and looked set up for a party.

"What's going on?" Macy asked.

Luke turned the light on and nearly fifty people jumped out and yelled, "Surprise!"

Macy stared at them for a moment and then looked at Luke. "What's going on?" Macy repeated.

Zoey and Alex ran up to her, wrapping her in a hug.

"We love you, Macy," Zoey said.

"Thanks, but what's this for? It's not my birthday."

"It's the anniversary of your return home," Alex said. "I thought we should celebrate. Zoey's the one who thought we should surprise you."

"It worked." Macy clutched her heart.

Other guests swarmed Macy, hugging her and expressing their gratitude for her safe return a year earlier. Macy teared up as people shared about how worried they had been for her, spending hours searching or handing out fliers. Some of the people she barely knew.

Luke's mom, Caroline, wrapped her arms around Macy. "I can't thank you enough for everything you and your family has done for us. We really wouldn't have been able to get back on our feet without you guys."

"And I never would have gotten away from Chester without Luke."

Caroline shook her head. "I don't know how I ever fell for everything Jonah and the community taught."

Luke hugged his mom. "You were trying to get us off the streets, and they offered you that and more."

Tears shone in her eyes. "Thanks, Luke. If I could go back in time, I would do so much differently."

Other people came up to Macy, wanting to talk. Caroline squeezed her hand. "We'll talk later."

When Macy finally had some space, she sat down at a table to breathe. Zoey brought over a plate full of cake and other sweets. Alex and Luke followed, carrying what looked like cups of punch.

"Did we surprise you?" Zoey asked, smiling.

"My heart hasn't returned to its normal speed yet."

Zoey grinned. "Good. That's what we were going for."

Valerie came to the table and handed little Ariana to Zoey, and then gave Macy a huge hug. "You've always been like a second daughter to me. I was so relieved when you were found safe and sound." She turned to Zoey. "Can you hold Ari for a few minutes?"

"Of course." Zoey snuggled Ariana.

A girl walked to the table. It took Macy a minute to realize who she was.

"Heather! What are you doing here?" Macy jumped out of the chair and gave her a hug. "How are you? I heard your grandparents adopted you."

Luke grabbed a chair from another table and motioned for Heather to sit.

"They did," Heather said. "It's so much nicer living with them."

"I bet," Macy said. "Are you guys staying at the farm?"

"You didn't hear?" asked Heather.

Macy shook her head.

"After they found out what Dad used the barn for, they were so disgusted that Grandpa sold the animals and burned it down. They thought they could live in the house, but they couldn't. Grandma nearly had a nervous breakdown every time she looked where the barn used to be. So they sold their home of forty-five years and moved into our old house."

Macy thought about that for a minute. A sense of relief swept through her as she thought about the barn burning up. "And you get to school with your friends?"

Heather nodded. "It's weird though, knowing that Dad was there with you and his new wife."

Macy gave her a hug. "I'm so sorry for everything he's put you through."

"And I you. You didn't do anything—you're not even related to him. You really didn't deserve any of it."

"You don't either. At least I got to come home to my entire family, and I brought a boyfriend with me."

"And you got a niece!" Zoey said, holding Ariana up. "Sorry. Couldn't help overhearing. So, how are you fitting back into society after being in that loony bin?"

"Zoey," Macy hissed.

Heather laughed. "No, it's fine. I call it the nut house. Luckily my grandparents have been so helpful. I've been talking to one of their church counselors, and I'm in martial arts. That's helping me release a lot of energy and regain some self-esteem. Plus my friends come over for sleepovers, like, all the time. I'm less jumpy now. Not quite normal, but I think I'm getting there."

"I know how you feel," Macy said. "If I didn't have these guys," she looked at Alex, Zoey, and Luke, "I don't know what I'd do. Homeschooling helps, even though a lot of the girls who bullied me have apologized. I really don't want to go back."

Luke wrapped an arm around her. "She's making a lot of progress. When we first met up after she came home, she didn't want to go anywhere alone. Now she's fine with it." He kissed the top of her head.

"Yeah," Zoey agreed. "She was having these anxiety attacks for a while, and it totally didn't help that whenever she went somewhere some idiot reporter would jump out from nowhere and ask her a million questions."

Heather shook her head. "I can't even imagine. Yeah, I was having panic attacks too. They suck."

Macy and Heather exchanged a knowing look.

"We really should keep in touch," Macy said. "Maybe even have some sleepovers. I'd love to spend some more time with George and Ingrid, too. You'd have fun with my friends."

"Oh, definitely," Zoey said. "I know how to throw a party."

Macy shook her head, smiling. She turned back to Heather. "Can I get you anything? Some punch or cake?"

"You're the guest of honor, you shouldn't—"

"You should be, too. Let me get you something."

"If you insist. Thanks."

Macy got up and headed for the refreshment table. She could hear Zoey and Alex talking with Heather. Before Macy got to the table, she saw George and Ingrid at the far end of the room. She decided to thank them for everything they had done, even though they hadn't realized that Macy wasn't Heather.

Had they not been at the farmhouse when they were, Macy might not have had the strength to keep fighting. It also meant the world to Macy that Ingrid had taught her to cook from scratch.

Before she reached the table, Macy noticed her dad off to the side talking with a pretty, younger dark-haired lady. She looked somewhat familiar. Maybe she was a neighbor or his coworker.

Macy was curious and took the long way to George and Ingrid, passing by her dad. Neither he nor the lady appeared to notice her.

The lady looked upset. "I just wanted to let you know, Chad."

"Are you sure you need to? Why not make sure—?"

"No. I'm leaving right after the party. I can't tell anyone where I'm going. If what I discovered is true, it's not safe for me at home anymore."

"Why don't you take the evidence to the authorities?"

"I can't. Dean's a dangerous man. I need to start over. I just wanted you to know before I disappeared."

Macy's dad saw her standing there. He waved her away. Obviously he didn't want her hearing the conversation. Macy shrugged and walked away.

She went to George and Ingrid and gave them hugs. "Thank you so much for being kind to me. I know you didn't know who I was…but it meant everything to me. I've even taught my mom how to cook a couple things from scratch."

Ingrid's face scrunched up like she was going to cry. "I wish I would have known. There's no way we would have let you stay there if we knew you were ripped from your family. Looking back, I felt that something was off, but Chester had convinced us that you were acting strange because your mom took off. I feel like such a fool."

Macy gave her another hug. "Don't. He had a lot of people tricked. How's Heather doing, really?"

"Good," said George. "Like you, she has a lot to recover from, but she's handling it like a champ."

Macy smiled. "I'm glad she has you guys."

"Oh," said Ingrid, pulling out her large handbag, "before I forget. Is this yours?" She pulled out Macy's teddy bear. The one that had gotten her through some rough nights—when Chester wasn't hiding it from her.

It must have somehow made its way from the community to the farmhouse.

Macy's eyes lit up. "My bear."

Ingrid handed it to her. "It was in Chester's things, but Heather had never seen it before. I thought it might be yours."

Macy hugged the bear and then talked with them for a few more minutes before she headed back to the table. Her parents joined them, and Macy looked around at everyone there. She was overwhelmed with how good things were. Everything was going to be okay. It really was.

Letter

Dear Chester,

I didn't think I would have the courage to write or send this letter, but here I am. It's been a year since we last saw each other, and you still haunt my dreams, but even that is lessening.

There were so many things I wanted to say (and scream) while I was with you. Mostly things that you already knew, but wouldn't let me say. I'm not Heather, never have been, and never will be. You know that as well as I do. The real Heather and I have become friends, actually. You lost her, and now you pretty much lost everything.

With more than two life sentences, you'll have a really long time to think about all the things you did to hurt so many people.

The only good that really came from you kidnapping and torturing me is that I got to meet Heather and Luke. Your daughter is doing well, but that's all I'm going to say. If you want to hear more about her, you'll have to hope she decides to ever talk to you again. It doesn't sound promising right now.

My counselor wanted me to write this letter. She didn't say I had to mail it, but I want to. You don't have to read it, I honestly don't care. I'm just glad for the chance to say what I need to. For a long time I hated you. Really hated you. Especially when you kidnapped me. But then I learned that it only ate away at me. My hate did nothing to you. I don't want to hate, so I'm letting it go.

But first, I have some questions for you. What makes you think you have the right to take someone from their family? Why do you think you're so special that you get to decide whether someone lives or dies? There's nothing special about you. You're a sick, sick man. I don't get it. Your parents are wonderful people. You had a beautiful family. Yet you gave it all up to control everyone.

I don't understand what could drive you to do all the things you did when you had everything in the world. But you know what? I'm done asking myself why. It would drive me crazy if I tried to make sense of it. There is no logic when it comes to you.

Actually, if you want to know the truth (and I doubt you do, because you hate the truth) I feel sorry for you. I've spent more time thinking about you than I care to admit. Go ahead and smirk. Think you've won. You haven't. I pity you, you poor excuse for a man.

Anyone who acts like you do obviously thinks he has no value. People who know they're worth something treat others well. You clearly know what a jerk you are, but instead of making yourself better you tried to force people to love you. You can't force love, especially when you're as horrible as you are. At one point, people loved you. Karla chose to marry you. Heather used to love you.

With this letter, I am letting you go. Letting go of the hold you have on me. Letting go of every memory of you. I'm done. It's over. You had a hold on me for a while, but no longer.

So goodbye, Chester.
Macy Mercer

Did you enjoy this trilogy? *There will be more to come from some of the side characters.*

Wondering what happened to Lydia? Find out in *Dean's List* as she runs from Dean's secret.

Rusty will have a story of his own also. Readers have asked for Luke to have a story, too.

Other books by Stacy Claflin

Gone series
Gone
Held
Over
Complete Trilogy

Now Available:
Dean's List (Lydia's story)

The Transformed Series
Deception (#1)
Betrayal (#2)
Forgotten (#3)
Silent Bite (#3.5)
Ascension (#4)
Duplicity (#5)
Sacrifice (#6)
Destroyed (#7)
Hidden Intentions (novel)
A Long Time Coming (Short Story)
Fallen (Novella)
Taken (Novella)

Seaside Hunters (Sweet Romance)
Seaside Surprises (Now Available)
Seaside Heartbeats (Coming Soon)
Seaside Dances (Coming Soon)
Seaside Kisses (Coming Soon)
Seaside Christmas (Coming Soon)

Other books
Chasing Mercy
Searching for Mercy

Visit StacyClaflin.com for details.

Sign up for new release updates.
stacyclaflin.com/newsletter

Want to hang out and talk about books? Join My Book Hangout:
facebook.com/groups/stacyclaflinbooks

and participate in the discussions. There are also exclusive giveaways,
sneak peeks and more. Sometimes the members offer opinions on book
covers too. You never know what you'll find.

Author's Note

Thanks so much for reading Over. I hope you've enjoyed the trilogy as much as I have. Many readers have expressed how much they enjoyed the story, and that means so much to me. I really believe that people can become better people as a result of difficult circumstances, and I loved watching the characters grow throughout the books.

If you enjoyed this book, please consider leaving a review wherever you purchased it. Not only will your review help me to better understand what you like—so I can give you more of it!—but it will also help other readers find my work. Reviews can be short—just share your honest thoughts. That's it.

Want to know when I have a new release? Sign up here (stacy-claflin.com/newsletter) for new release updates. You'll even get a free book!

I've spent many hours writing, re-writing, and editing this work. I even put together a team who helped with the editing process. As it is impossible to find every single error, if you find any, please contact me through my website and let me know. Then I can fix them for future editions.

Thank you for your support!

~Stacy

If you enjoyed the Gone trilogy, you may enjoy my Transformed series. You can read the first book for *free* at most online retailers.

About:

What if your whole life was a lie?

Alexis Ferguson thinks she has everything figured out, but has no idea how wrong she is. Set up on a blind date, she meets a gorgeous stranger and feels that she's known him her entire life, but she has never seen him before.

He awakens in her long-forgotten dark memories, and now she must face the one who ordered her death years ago. Will she learn to use her strange new powers in time to save herself? Will she let him help her? Should she trust him?

Download links
stacyclaflin.com/books/the-transformed-series

Made in the USA
Middletown, DE
14 January 2017